Two Knights in London

by

Paul Boon

GOODHILL BOOKS
England
2016

The book cover shows Riley Wilkin as Edward
and Lawrie Wilkin as Richard.
Photos by Rebecca Challis Photography.

ISBN 978-1539510697

All rights reserved.

This book is sold subject to the condition that it shall not, by way of trade or otherwise, be lent, resold, hired out, or otherwise circulated without the publisher's prior consent in any form of binding or cover other than that in which it is published and without a similar condition including this condition being imposed on the subsequent publisher.

In 1483 the twelve years old, forcefully deposed King Edward V, along with his younger brother Richard of Shrewsbury, disappeared from their rooms in the Tower of London despite heavy guard. Since then there has been no definite evidence to show what became of the two princes.

There have been many suspects, not least their uncle King Richard the third, but their fate remains one of history's many mysteries.

This story allows for the possibility of magic and a world known only to a very few. It begins during a time when men still believed in wizards and the power of spells. A time of treachery and Chivalry, when good men fought against evil. A time of honour and betrayal. A Time of Heroes.

Apart from the two princes all the characters in this story are fictitious and are not meant to reflect any actual person either living or dead.

CHAPTERS

1483

Bewitched

Yesterday's Now

When in Rome

The Need to Know

Emotion's Eve

Morning After

Encounters

Kings and Stuff

For the People

End of the Beginning

For Archie
(A fellow writer)

Edward V was born 2 November 1470 and became King at the age of 12 when his father died in 1483. While he was staying in the Tower of London, waiting for his coronation, his uncle had him imprisoned in the White Tower. He was never seen again.

For an illustration of Edward, I chose young actor Riley Wilkin who seems to have similar qualities to the real Edward (according to the limited amount we know of Edward).

So, a big thanks to Riley Wilkin for his inspiration, helping to paint a picture of Edward during the writing process.

Richard of Shrewsbury, Duke of York, was born 17 August 1473 – younger brother to Edward V. When Edward was imprisoned in the Tower of London, Richard was with his mother at Westminster Abbey. He was taken to The Tower under pretence that he would be returned to his mother later. After two months, he and Edward were never seen again.

Little is known of the actual personality of Richard but he would have had similar coaching to his brother, as heir presumptive.

A big thanks to young actor Lawrie Wilkin whose image helps to paint a more colourful picture of Richard.

1483

A storm was raging. It seemed that the sun had been captured by the spirit of doom which had turned night into even darker night, with rain enough to wash away the tears of a million lifetimes. It pelted against the castle walls. Thunder echoed against the darkness and then, suddenly, there it was! Something shrouded within a purple mist. Flickering torches growing closer and a desperate feel of foreboding.

Why were his feet so heavy? Was the ground sinking? He struggled to break free, to pull himself up, to face whatever was approaching. Then he heard his brother shouting, pleading, but he was stuck fast. Some form of magic! Rain was turning the floor into quicksand, and he was being sucked in. A moving shadow in the darkest corner of the night, but he saw, and almost caught hold of, his brother's hand as a skeleton of a wagon whisked him away.

Then he was being smothered. Strong hands were holding in place. A voice, muffled, desperate. His own voice. His own terror. The purple mist turned into a deep red fog, then like a fiery furnace, engulfing him, drawing him deeper in. His brother's voice like a hollow echo. He tried to grab on to the burning crevice. Then, like a dagger to his heart, he was tossed against a terrifying nothingness. Dark. Empty.

Then he was awakened by the sound of a key in the lock.

There was no red fog; just a faint hint of moonlight through the window. He could see his brother sleeping beside him. The door opened. He watched as two hooded men entered. One lit a torch beside the doorway.

"Who are you?" asked Edward. "Where are the usual guards?"

"We are your guards this night," said the second man. "And your escort." He tossed Edward's clothing to him. "Waken your brother and dress yourselves. There is not much time."

"I am a Royal Prince," said Edward. "I never dress myself."

"Do as I say."

"Where is Miles? My servant."

"No more words."

Edward gave the escorts a disapproving glare. "Our Uncle shall hear of this." Even as he spoke he knew his cause was lost. Gradually, his trusted friends and servants had been dismissed, and the only person with the power to do that was their Uncle. He gently shook his brother who looked around vacantly for a moment.

"What is it?" asked Richard.

"We must get up," Edward told him.

"Why?"

"I think we are being moved."

"Happy birthday!" said the escort, quite sneeringly, to Richard.

The younger boy knew that the sentiment was not genuine. Who could have a happy birthday imprisoned in a cold tower. There had been no warmth of any kind in this place since they had arrived. They both changed their clothing, under the watch of their escorts. Edward felt his skin goosebumping but he tried not to let his foreboding show.

They followed the torchlight down the dark stairway and along the empty corridors. Edward noticed the absence of guards. Even in the smaller hours there were usually guards posted at key points. "Where are we going?" he demanded.

No answer. He stopped walking but was pushed forward by an escort. They were nearing the forecourt and he could see a covered wagon waiting. And even greater unease gripped him and he stopped again. "No." He said. "Enough!"

His escort took hold of him and gagged his mouth. Richard gave a slight whimper as he was also held and gagged. Both struggled but were not strong enough to resist. They were manhandled into the wagon. If anyone awoke to see the wagon leaving, they would just assume the wagon was a bit unstable. Edward guessed that the guards at the gate must had been told to let it pass because nobody came to inspect the inside. It was a rickety old cart which bobbled over the cobbles, so the journey was quite uncomfortable.

Richard was sobbing silently, his face awash with tears, his head held against the floor. He thought of his mother, the good times at Ludlow Castle, his dog, their plans for his tenth birthday celebration. The wagon smelled of rotted wood and cabbage. His escort smelled of stale sweat. He could not see his bother but he sensed his presence, the was the only shred of comfort he had.

Edward had secretly expected something to happen. He had prepared himself, the best he could, reading scripture, praying, trying to believe that there had to be some purpose for everything. When his brother had been imprisoned with him, he was convinced that it was a good sign but, as days passed and their familiar companion began to be removed, all his hopes had faded.

Now Edward remembered the dream. The wagon. His brother, The hands. His feelings. The fiery furnace! The darkness! Death? Was this to be his final dream of all? Where was the God that he had read about? He still believed but he did not understand. Maybe true understanding could never be had until after death.

From his place on the floor of the cart, Edward could see one small star in the night sky, between the clouds. He wondered about stars, how they existed, what they meant. How far away was this star? Was it really in

Heaven? He felt a drop of rain on the wind. He wished he could just roll out of the wagon and get lost in the trees and grass. He knew that he could not escape without his brother, and was plunged back into hopelessness again.

The wagon hit a rock and Edward's escort cursed. A brief glimpse of a figure running across the track was all the moment allowed, but it gave Edward a strange optimism. He remembered how his father that said that help sometimes comes in ways least expected. He wondered about the person, who they were, where they were going, and he wished he could taste the same freedom.

∽

The ground was indeed rugged but the runner was young and nimble. He took one look back at the wagon and thought he caught a brief twinkle from an eye before it evaporated into the night. He could not be sure, but the road coming north from The Tower had been rarely used in the deepest hours of the night since the curfew. He looked up at the remains of a gibbet and shuddered.

The rain was still light. So far he had not encountered any ghosts or footpads but the moon was far from full and the lamps of city too dim to comfort him. He pressed on. Not far to go now. A rabbit surprised him from the ground, and a tawny owl fluttered above. He held a wooden cross close to his chest. He recognised a lightning tree and knew he was near the checkpoint.

"Is that you, Steven?" come a boy's voice, sudden and startling.

The runner, Steven, sighed. "Adam, don't creep up like that."

"I wasn't."

"Where are they?"

"Come." Adam led the way to a couple of riders concealed by the night. He was small, just a boy of nine years but proud to be the trusted page of his cousin Sir Ralph Eden of York. He looked up at the knight who was clad in casual chainmail. "No word from Harold yet, Sire, but here's Steven."

Sir Ralph took a bite of an apple and passed the rest of it to Adam. "What news, young Steven?"

"Just an old wagon, Sire, but ... there was something in it, low down. Possibly people."

Another knight, Sir Robert L'aselle of Shrewsbury, came more into the moonlight. "Which road did they take?"

"Towards the marshland, Sire."

The bell at St. Giles struck three. "Tis a curious time to be visiting the marshland," said Sir Ralph. "Unless the purpose is dishonourable." He heard a sound close by and turned to face a young man who staggered into the clearing. He was injured in the arm. "What happened to you, Harold?"

The youth had been running and took a few breaths before speaking. "Word from the castle, Sire. Edward is being moved tonight. The signal was short and I was pursued but I was too quick for them to follow."

"Not too quick to be caught by an arrow," noted Sir Robert.

"It just nicked my arm," said Harold.

"We should go see this wagon." said Sir Ralph. "Whether it carries cabbage or our rightful King. If it is our King, pray we carry this night well."

"Indeed," agreed Robert, adjusting his chainmail. "One more day and we could have had more of an army, but I suspect that our plans were discovered. Treachery and deceit I think."

"I shall come too," said Adam. "I am quick and light and you will need all the help you can get."

"This will not be practice," assured Ralph. "We may find that we are against a hundred men, each with skills equal to ours."

"Each a giant, ten feet tall," suggested Sir Robert.

"Each with four heads and swords of ice," added Sir Ralph, with a smirk.

"Then you will need every man that you can find. Me and Steven and Harold are good followers of King

Edward," announced Adam, with resolve. "And if we free the King and Richard Prince there will be seven of us. Seven on the right side are better than a hundred on the wrong. Even if they be giants."

"It would still be suicide," said Robert. "Have you no sense?"

Ralph put a hand on Adam. "My cousin, I admire your courage, and I love you dearly but you are no match for such opponents. Once morning comes you will ride to your father's estate and wait until he feels it is safe. Do not follow us to the marshland. I want your promise on that."

Adam wanted to protest but knew his own limitations. "They mean to kill Edward," he said hopelessly. I know they do."

"And we intend to stop them," said Robert. "We are knights who swore to protect the King and his family. We shall defend them or die trying."

"No matter how long it takes?" asked Adam.

"No matter how long." confirmed Robert. "You have the right spirit, young Adam. You shall make a fine knight one day."

Adam blushed slightly. Sir Ralph reached down and kissed his cousin. "Be strong, my cousin. Right is on our side."

The two knights steered their horses to the road and set off in pursuit of the wagon.

Their gags were removed and the two Royal boys were set down on the ground, surrounded by flaming torches. Edward looked around at the scattering of people. Monks? No, not truly. There was a slight scent of incense in the wind but not quite the same as in a church. He felt Richard clutching on to him, and then his crucifix was ripped from his neck. The night was suddenly cold. He wanted to wake up but he knew, in his breaking heart, that this nightmare was real.

Their escorts pushed them roughly forward. Richard fell over and whimpered but Edward helped him to he feet. "Don't let them see your fear," he said, trying to deny the tightening within his own chest."

"Treat them gently," said a man wearing a red robe. A priest? A Wizard? "There is no need for extra unpleasantness."

Edward, despite his terror, faced the man. "Who are you? What right have you to do this? I am your rightful King."

"Your uncle is King," said the man, softly.

"My uncle is a usurper." Edward looked around at the hooded figured. "I have an army ready to restore me. Show your faces and prove that you are not just cowards hiding in the night."

"Your army is merely a fantasy," said the same soft voice. "Those few followers you had are lost in the shadows."

"So now you plan to murder us?" asked Edward.

"Murder is an ugly word." The man nodded to the escorts. "Bring them closer. They will not run. They have no place to run to."

The boys were place in a circle. Edward could feel Richard trembling as they clung together. *'Witchcraft!'* thought Edward. He remembered the fire from his dream. He kissed his brother and expected the worst. They both closed their eyes. It should not be long now, then they would learn what Heaven was like. Maybe their father will be there to greet them. Edward realised he was crying. He was angry at himself for showing such weakness, but did that really matter now?

Shouting! *'Even now they torment us!'* said a frightened voice inside him. Soon the ground would give way and they would be sucked into nothingness, like in nightmare. He was holding his brother up, sobbing with him. He dared a quick glance at the scene. Some kind of ritual? Some confusion? He saw purple mist; the priest, wizard or whatever he was, hands held high. Edward was feeling faint. Was this how it ends?

Sir Ralph? Was Sir Ralph in heaven with sword in his hand? Now he could hear Richard, crying, pleading. He crushed him close. Let them enter Heaven together. He could see two knights now, among the stars, fighting against demons. Swords clashed. Then darkness! Silence! Then nothing!

∽

"I can smell the evil in this place," said Sir Robert as they approached.

The two knights dismounted, tethered their horses and crept closer. They could see the wagon, now empty, and they could see the hooded gathering. Then they saw the boys, looking more like terrified children than Royal princes. Ralph felt himself flush with anger, but he knew they must choose their timing carefully. Who were these people? What were their skills in combat? The smoke from the torches helped shelter their progress, and all eyes were focused on the young King who was speaking.

Swords at ready, they saw the boys taken closer to a circle. "Witchcraft!" breathed Sir Robert with distaste. There was a dozen hooded people around the circle. The boys had closed their eyes. A purple mist had descended. It was time! The knights plunged into the area and attacked the gathering.

Two hoods were cut down before the others realised anything was happening. The others were quick to respond. Soon steel clashed against steel. These were not monks or witches. They were men at arms. The two knights were a match, but only just. Sir Robert found himself taking on three together. It was only his speed and agility what gave him the edge.

Sir Ralph was closer to the main circle. He thought that his King was praying but then he was distracted by his opponents. What made him the better fighter was his determination to save the boys. "In the King's name!" he called, as he plunged his sword into a particularly annoying foe. He narrowly avoided being made a ghost and sent his opponent fleeing.

Where was the man in red? He was just there, in front of them. Or maybe not. The rush of battle can play tricks in the most experienced knight. The purple mist was fading slightly as Sir Ralph realised that his fight seemed to be over. Only two of the hooded group were left standing. Sir Robert seemed to be coping with them well, but the King and Prince Richard were gone. As Sir Ralph neared the centre of the circle his head began to spin. He backed off and turned in time to see Sir Ralph's final opponent running away.

"The King is gone!" Ralph told him.

"Aye, witchcraft!" said Robert. "Mayhap that purple mist is hiding the King beyond."

Ralph did not relish the prospect of any encounter with magic but he saw no alternative. "No doubt it's some form of trickery. Should we both risk it or just one?" He saw that the colour was now fading fast within the circle and knew that there was only one answer. With only a brief glance between them, the two knights, with swords at the ready, rushed at the purple mist – and disappeared.

Bewitched

The sky was clear. Dawn was in full bloom with orange streaks parting the waking eye-lids of a fresh day. A light breeze tickled his golden hair. Edward thought that it had been a dream, or nightmare, until he realised that he was outside. Trees dotted a small field and, beyond, were buildings that were strange to him. The air was strange also. In some ways sweeter; in some ways cleaner. Was that thunder, despite the clear sky? A lingering, rumbling. He sat up, checked himself, saw his brother some few feet away, sleeping.

A scrap of coloured paper, smoother than any he had seen before and with a curious texture was on the grass nearby. He picked it up but did not understand the writing on it. Then a crack of thunder, louder and more ferocious than the others. It woke his brother and the two boys were soon cowering, then running, though they did not know where to. Then they saw it. A dragon? It soared above them, red eyes and pale body, shimmering, high, high above the tree tops. Hopefully too high to notice them.

The younger brother, clinging to a tree, breathed hard. Woken to a hazy terrifying reality where grass and sky blurred into a hollow nothingness as he gasped for understanding. The elder brother watched the dragon slowly disappear into the distance. He had heard tales and such things but he was always reluctant to believe, until now. Then he saw a man in a kind of single chariot but with both wheels on the same side. The man studied the boys quietly as he passed by. Slowly, the rumbling seemed to grow into a deafening cacophony.

Richard stared at the new world and then allowed his brother to come into focus. "Where are we?" he asked feebly, "What's happening? Where are we? Where is this place?"

"I don't know," said Edward, truthfully. "I think we are alive but maybe bewitched."

"*Bewitched!*" breathed Richard in horror. "In Hell?"

"No! Not Hell. I won't believe that," said Edward. "We've done nothing to deserve Hell. That was a wizard. The purple mist! He did something. A spell of something."

Richard collapsed more wretchedly than before. Edward held him. "Courage my brother. We live. We are surrounded by strangeness but we are alive."

"But what can we do?" asked Richard. "Where can we go? Who will be our champion?"

"I'll think of something." Edward sat down beneath the tree branches with his brother. "They were going to kill us! I do not understand what magic was used. We survived and can take some comfort in that."

"This is a fearful place. The ground murmurs like a wasp nest" He took a better look at his surroundings; benches, some kinds of buckets and a few signs at the side of a road or driveway. They both carefully approached one of the signs.

"The words are English but the spelling is odd," said Edward. "Possibly that new English that we were told about. This says that we are in Weavers Fields. I do not know that place." He glanced with some horror at the rows of tall buildings across the road. A mighty castle? Which kingdom? "Horseless carriages!" An endless parade of them. An endless monotony.

They sat on one of the benches and watched in silence, each with their private misgivings and fears. People passed in growing numbers, wearing unfamiliar fashions, many, it seemed, from different lands. All seemed to have a particular purpose. They were in a city like none other they had witnessed. The mixture of sounds and emotions overwhelmed them. Two boys out of time. Both wiped tears from their eyes.

Edward was the first to regain any composure. "We must see if there is a church." He said. "If this indeed is not Hell then there may be a priest who will shelter us."

∽

The purple mist had subsided. Now a strange orange night lay before the two knights. But which realm were they in? Unfamiliar buildings surrounded them, and a continuous rumble bothered them deeply. They gripped their swords and lay back to back prepared to do battle against whatever came. There was no sign of the King or Prince Richard, their abductors or, indeed, of the wizard. Something unimaginable had happened. They had both heard of acts of wizardry but this was their first personal experience.

A fox wandered across their path. Ralph scanned the field and the nearby metal fence, and what looked like a manor house beyond. He motioned for Robert to follow and they made their way cautiously towards the manor. Was this the stronghold of the wizard? Was it a mere a fox that had just passed by or was it a demon in disguise? They had no idea what lay ahead but they were loyal knights prepared to find and defend the royal princes.

Over the bushes and metal fence they studied the wall and wooden gate. Lamps lit their way but each lamp was on a tall post and seemed to be powered by some means that they did not understand. No surprise in the realm of wizards. No lights shone from the manor. The small gate was well bolted.

Some quiet voices could be heard. The knights followed the sound and saw a kind of coach without horses. The men were inside. Guards? If truly guards, they were going to get a swift despatch. One got out and placed a cap on his head. No armour or visible weapon.

"Surrender now, or meet your end," called Ralph.

The other 'guard' stepped out of the coach also. "What's this then? Practice for a pageant? Why you don't put those swords down and we'll give you a lift to where you can sleep it off."

"He toys with us," smiled Robert.

The first 'guard' began to mutter into his hand. More wizardry? The knights wasted no more time. They each took on a 'guard' who had some kind of magic fighting stick which grew longer within seconds. Ralph took advantage of the one who was muttering. Flipped him over and hammered his sword on the 'guard's' shoulder. Robert pinned the other to the coach. Then the magic sticks came into play. The 'guards' were stronger than had first seemed, so the fight lasted longer than expected. Ralph overcame his quickest then turned in time to see the other spray Robert with a magic potion which seemed to blind him. Ralph took a small dagger from his tunic and shot it over the coach to down the remaining 'guard'.

Repeating wailing, like a troupe of banshees began to grow closer. Ralph recovered his dagger from the 'guard' who appeared to be still alive. He quickly helped Robert to his feet and they fled back across the metal fence. Magically, bright lights with roving beams began to search the ground before them. Shouts from several directions. The two knights, unable to find adequate cover among the bushes, headed for the streets.

A high walled yard gave them some temporary shelter while Robert recovered himself from the pain that had cut him through like a blade. Not blood; more like internal fire which was slowly fading. A blue flickering light like an evil spirit cruised the streets near them. Another light came on in an upper window of the building they were hiding behind. A curtain was drawn. The knights held their breath as a woman looked out.

Dogs barked in several houses and more lights come on.

"We cannot fight the whole of Hades!" said Robert.

"We can if Heaven is our award," replied Ralph. "And it's possible we must if we are to find and free the King." He had kept one of the magic sticks. "This doesn't seem to be a match for our swords. If it has any magic in it, it's beyond me."

"Maybe the only magic is in the way it lengthens."

"That's no magic. More like a child's toy."

A loud, long, heavy rumbling made them wonder if the earth was shattering. It lasted for less than a minute and was followed by more shouts. Ralph climbed up to look over the wall at the opposite of the yard to the gate. The only way forward was up through another metal fence, and then another climb, a kind of mound. Then a long drop to a narrow street, but this narrow street was less lit. They moved quickly along a line of horseless coaches, hoping that this would lead away from the searchers.

They found themselves facing a tunnel deep in the wizard's city. A deafening roar made them block their ears. Again the earth rumbled. The knights saw an old man emerge from the shadows, but then he seemed to be gone. No purple mist but, they were sure, this was similar magic. Then the old was visible again. They prepared themselves, but saw in his eyes only confusion and slight fear. Was that part of the trickery?

Another blue light, flashing beyond the tunnel. The old man beckoned them to follow him. When they hesitated he waved frantically. "Come. Come. They will find you like they found the others. Come. Come."

Something inside them made them follow him through a dark passage to a boarded up building. Words were scrawled on the wood door post. It was not clear if it had been a shop or house, but the level of dust and cobwebs suggested that it had been vacant for a long time. There was no furniture as such, just a few wooden crates and a pile of rags. Words were also casually scrawled on the walls inside. *'Woody Wuz Ere'*

"They won't find us here. This place is haunted you know." The man had a mad twinkle to his smile. "Sit down." He cleared rubbish from the crates. "Sit down.

I've been hiding here for ages … ages …" His voice trailed and, suddenly, he was lost in a foggy memory, until he recovered himself. "They think I'm dead but, yes, sometimes they wonder, because I make them wonder. Like they wonder about you, now."

"Who are you?" asked Ralph.

"I ask that too. Often! I used to know … when I was younger but … it was so long ago. I forget. Yes, I forget most things but occasionally I remember things." He rummaged in the rubbish and found a tin. "I have sardines. I like sardines. You must be hungry."

"Who were you hiding from?" asked Robert. "The wizard's guards?"

"Guards? No, not them … but maybe someone!" he opened a tin. "Maybe someone as mad as the most mad." He stopped and tittered then looked Ralph in the face. "I haven't been to the toilet for fifty years!"

Ralph gave Robert a silent stare.

The old man sobered suddenly. "You'll be mad too once you've been here long enough. It took many years. They said I was mad. They locked me up, but I got way. Be sure they don't lock you up too."

"We have no intention of being locked up," said Ralph.

A light flashed by, reflected in the dusted windows. "They are looking for you, and they will find you unless you change your garb." He looked them over and admired their swords. "I … I think I used to have … but nobody dresses like that here, and they'll arrest you just for carrying those weapons. Then they will lock you up, especially if you use them." His suddenly eyes gleamed. "Hey, did you kill anyone?"

Robert pointed his sword at the old man's chest. "I don't think we killed them, but I'm not sure that we shouldn't kill you. You are too strange, old mad. Maybe there is a darker magic in you, and this madman scene is just an act."

"No. No." The old man backed against the wall. "I mean you no harm. Please … I saved you!"

"What is this place? In who's realm?"

"Who's realm?" The old man gawped at them. "Well, The Queen's realm ... now. This is England."
"Which Queen?" asked Ralph.
"Queen Elizabeth. Look ..." he picked up a newspaper from the floor and showed it to Robert. "See? Ninety years old. Ninety!"
"What manner of parchment is this?" Robert handed it to Ralph. "How come such paintings upon it?"
"It's only a newspaper. It's how we read about things happening." The old man circled the two knights, studying them closely again. "Tomorrow we might read about you. We ..." He sat down on a crate. "There is something ... or nothing ... that I almost remember but then lose it again. It's them needles!"
"Just take things easy, Old Man," said Ralph. He struggled with the wording in the newspaper. "Elizabeth is Queen but has reached ninety. So maybe the wizard has played with time and has stolen about fifty years. Tell me, old man, who is next in line to the throne?"
"That would be Charles," he said.
"Charles of France?" asked Robert.
"No, Prince Charles, the Queen's son."
The knights glanced at each other. "So Elizabeth had another son? What of Edward and Richard? And tell us how King Richard died, and how did Elizabeth take the crown from him? Was there a mighty battle?"
The barrage of questions seemed to confuse the old man. "I ... I do not ... Edward, yes, Edward went into the theatre I think. Richard ..."
"Edward is a player?" gasped Robert. "That I cannot believe. Nobody would give up their kingdom to become a player."
"But Edward lives?" asked Ralph.
"Yes, he lives. I think he is the youngest son would most likely not be King anyway."
"Youngest?" asked Robert. "What you say? Elizabeth had more children and another one was named Edward? Did the first Edward die?"

The old man put his head in his hands. "I don't know. I don't know. Maybe I remember things wrong."

"At least," remarked Ralph. "These last few years have seen changes, and a new breed of painters who can capture a likeness like no others." He handed the newspaper back to the old man. "But our Edward and Prince Richard must be in this time with us. We must seek an audience with the Queen and try to set things right."

"Agreed," said Robert.

"But ..."

"There are no buts, old man."

"I might be old. I might get confused, but I do know that if you try to see the Queen, with or without swords, you will be arrested. Blue lights! Remember? If it has been fifty years, or not, you cannot just swan in and demand to be heard." He swayed and almost fell off his crate, but Robert steadied him. "I think ..."

The old man fainted away so Robert rested him on a pile of rags. "The old man is not such a fool as I thought," he said.

"Indeed."

"So what now? Lay low and wait to see what tomorrow brings?" Robert sighed. "It is not how I like to work, but we need to plan."

∽

"I do not like way the people stare at us," said Richard. "We look too different."

"Of course we are different," said Edward. "We are Royal!"

They both were wearing stockings and tunics which suited their princely status in 1483 but both were aware that this place was unusual. If they had truly been bewitched then it could be that everyone around them was dressed and behaving as normal but that the spell made them think otherwise. Edward was trying to put a brave face on everything but he was tingling with fright inside. He was born to be King. He should be King, but he was still just a boy and, now, without a champion.

The most terrifying moment so far had been the howling cave mouth which had caused the boys to flee. A magic snake thing had followed them, roaring, along the road until they had turned down to a short road where the snake thing lost them. They had rested where the road came to a stop. Many of the horseless coaches were travelling close to the cave but, here, there were just sitting silently. Both boys had quickly decided that the coaches were harmless, once the initial surprise has worn off, but how many other surprises would this new world bring?

They clung to each other. Edward could feel Richard trembling but, while their surroundings were amazing, the boys had not been harmed. Was this a sign of encouragement? Was there still a way out of this underworld? The sun was fully awake now and the air was warm. So different from then they had travelled by night away from the tower. But does a sunny day make everything alright?

Now Edward studied a building set back from the others. He had a strong hope that it was a church but the entrance must be at the other side. He linked arms with Richard and they followed a path which led them to the main gate. Edward gave silent thanks to God. If there was a church then not all hope was lost. Beside the gate were the words ST MATTEW'S CHURCH. He brushed a fresh tear from his eye.

"What if Shaa has persuaded people here against you?" asked Richard, lightly gloomily.

Edward hesitated only slightly then put a reassuring hand on his younger brother. "Then I shall try to persuade them otherwise. We never were bastard children!"

An Asian woman stopped before them and smiled at their attire. "Is there a special event this week?" she asked Edward.

"We have come to speak to the priest," he told her.

"There'll be no priest here at this time of morning." She said. "it's all locked up until someone comes to open it."

"How long to wait?"

"Maybe an hour until a warden arrives."

"Is your husband a merchant?" asked Richard, considering her appearance.

"No dear, he works in the city." She stroked the texture of his tunic. "That is well made. Lovely quality. Did your mother make it?"

Richard just quietly shook his head.

"Well, you both look awesome. Do you mind if I take a couple of pics?"

She did so but neither of the boys what that meant. They watched her disappear into one of the buildings opposite then sat on a bench in the grounds to wait. Richard wiped another tear from his eye. Edward put a hand around his brother. "It'll be better now that we are going to see a priest."

"It's not really that," Richard told him. "It's just, when that woman spoke, they were the first kind words since we were imprisoned in the White Tower."

Yesterday's Now

There was much for the knights to consider. The old man was still dozing on the rags but they spoke in near whispers anyway. There was no, in their minds, that the wizard had shifted time. But what of the Royal boys? Had they also been transported, not just to the same place but the same time? They each felt terribly ill at ease, and slightly awed. They were knights and known combat in various degrees, but this was a lot to take in.

"Edward is no fool," said Ralph, "But he is still a boy."

"And our true King," reminded Robert. "I can say that now. Even if King Richard did not order their deaths he took no steps to prevent it. I shall not mourn his demise."

"Nor shall I." Ralph had been going through things in his mind. "Edward is very devoted to his faith. That makes me think he would try to find a church as soon as possible. If this is truly England and not some magical realm, there must be a church somewhere local. That is where we should start to search."

"Agreed!" Robert took another look at their ragged, dusty, cobweb covered surroundings. The dawn was breaking and the city was becoming more alive. Sounds echoed, some familiar but many strange. The window looked out at a tall brick wall but, above that, could be seen tall rooftops. The rumbling had become as white noise; a mere backdrop to weirdness.

A shape in the twilight made Robert grip his sword. "Someone comes!"

Ralph joined him at the window and they each watched a woman come quietly along the passage towards the doorway.

Her name was Megan. She walked in unannounced as, apparently, was her want, and lit up a cigarette. Her manner was brisk, straightforward and, despite her shambolic appearance she had an air of confidence. She mostly ignored the knights for the first few minutes, bringing an assortment of goods out from her clothing and concealing them in certain places in the building. Under her mass of dark hair, she looked like she was maybe in her late thirties.

"So you're the ones everyone's talking about!" Megan sat on a bench and studied the knights. "I don't want to know who you really are. Anyone who sticks it to the man are okay by me." She took a long drag on her cigarette.

"There are many people searching for us?" asked Ralph.

"Not so much that you'd notice but no doubt you'll be in the news. The local twitter will be all about you for about half a day but, these days, people have a short attention span." She reached up and felt his tunic and chain mail. "What's with this though? Something to do with those conquest event at The Tower?"

Robert saw that the old man was tittering again. "We have two friends, boys, who we need to find," He told Megan. "They are lost and may be in trouble. We are wasting time sitting here!"

"Maybe," she said. "I don't know what your story is and, as I said, I don't really care. I survive by keeping to my own business. But I can tell you something for sure. If you go into the open dressed like that, they'll pick you up for sure."

"So, how are we supposed to dress? Like him?" He nodded to the old man.

"Do you have any money?"

"Money?" asked Ralph.

"Dosh, readies, cash, folding stuff. Silver and Gold!"

"Yes," Ralph took a small pouch from his tunic and showed some coins to Megan.

She picked up one Half Ryal and looked at closely. She bit on it and tested it in her mouth. "I haven't seen any of these in a long time, and in such good condition." She gave the knights a curious glance. "If these are forgeries then they are very good. And I can't see the point in forging such old coins; they would never be accepted as genuine ... unless ..."

"Unless what?" asked the old man who was gawping.

She studied the knights again. "This is either a massive, expensive con or ..." She stopped short and considered the evidence. "These could be from an unearthed stash, or there's something very unusual about you guys."

The old man laughed like a rusty hinge.

"The coins are real. They are mine." Ralph assured her.

"And worth a packet in today's money!" said Megan." If you let me, I know someone who will give new money to these old coins. No questions asked."

"All of them?" Asked Ralph.

"Well," Megan selected three coins and jingled them. "I guess it's best to not push things too much. Three will do. Then I can buy you new clothes. I'll keep a commission. Fair is fair! Then you will have walking about money."

The old man admired the swords again. "And I'll keep your swords here under cover. You can't take them with you when you search."

Robert pointed his sword at the old man again. "You had better keep them safe if you want to be safe yourself." He sheathed the sword again. "For the moment I will keep it ready. Who knows what this day shall bring."

∽

It was not music, nor even a chant. Edward and Richard watched as a horseless coach stopped by the gate and a slim man, youthful, clean shaven, seemed to wait until the sound had faded before getting out. He pressed his thumb and lights on the corners of the coach flashed. The coach made a beep sound and the young man approached the church entrance. He saw the boys and smiled.

"Are you waiting to come in, or just resting there?" His voice was friendly.

Edward looked him over. "Are you a priest?" he asked.

"No, I'm one of the wardens. Are you on your way to the Tower?"

Both boys flinched slightly but Edward tried to ignore negative images. "We have been in the tower," he said flatly. "Now I would like to see the priest."

"You are early starters," said the young man, unlocking the church door. "The priest will be here later. We don't actually have morning prayer today but you are welcome to come in. We'd love it if the church could be left open all the time but, unfortunately, it's just not realistic. Maybe one day."

The church was bright and airy compared to any others the boys had been in. They both crossed their chests on entering then marvelled at the modern design before taking seats at the back. The church had good acoustics. Edward remembered the better moments from the services he had attended. He knelt for a while and breathed softly, saying a prayer for his late father, a prayer for his mother and one for each of his sisters. Richard just stayed quiet, reflecting.

Edward was dreading confession, trying to explain his current feelings to a priest. Could he even trust all priests? What if something he says caused him to be arrested again? But how could he not go to confession? As King, or even as a prince, he had an example to set. He felt Richard's hand on his and he pressed it reassuringly.

After their solemn moments they explored the building. There was a rack with papers which the boys found fascinating even though the writing and spelling took some concentration. Richard was interested in the pictures of people, especially children and their odd clothing. He tried to imagine himself in their costumes. How the pictures were made was a mystery to him. He assumed that it was some kind of magic, over which he had no power, but he did not felt threatened by it. In many ways it was like remembering forgotten dreams.

The warden had gone through one of the doors at the back. Richard glanced at his brother and was surprised that Edward was looking quite ill. He had gone deathly pale and was clutching a piece of paper. "Are you not well?" Richard asked him.

Edward felt cold deep inside, like he'd been stabbed by an icicle. The church, the candles, the cross, the pulpit and even Richard seemed to be spinning around him. He was looking at the paper but also not looking at it. Lies! But maybe not lies. Maybe worse. He had to get out. Run ... but to where? He stumbled out of the church, his new world blurred by tears.

Richard followed him, worried and surprised.

Edward saw the railings at the border of the church yard. He hated the railings. He kicked at them. He clung to them but then collapsed against them. He hated crying. He was too old to cry, but now he wondered why it mattered. He forced himself to read the piece of paper again, but it was real enough. "Oh God," he wept. He saw his brother and grabbed on to him, gasping.

"What it is?" asked Richard "What happened?"

"It's all gone," spluttered Edward. "Everything! Everyone! Oh God!"

Richard plucked the piece of paper from his brother's hand and straightened it so that he could read it properly. It was in the form of an announcement that King Richard, the third England, was dead. He read the heading twice and felt torn emotions. Their uncle was dead, but how many times in the last few weeks had he wished for that to happen? He hugged his brother even tighter. "Uncle is dead! You are King!"

"No," groaned Edward.

"Yes!"

"No!" Edward wiped his eyes and tried to compose himself. "Read it properly."

Richard gazed at his older brother and then read the piece of paper fully.

"Look at the date." cried Edward, hopelessly. "We are dead. Mother is dead. Everyone is dead. We are indeed in Hell."

"No. It's wrong. That's not possible."

"I am not King. We are dead. Ghosts!"

"Shut up, brother. You said yourself we don't deserve to be dead." He put a hand on his own chest and then grabbed his brother's hand and pushed it against Edward's chest. "Listen," he ordered. "Feel it. Blood in our bodies. We cannot be dead!"

"How do you know what death is like? Maybe all ghosts just believe they are still alive."

"Brother." Richard held Edward in front of him and looked him deep in the eyes. "You are my life. You are my strength. I love you. This cannot be right."

A flicker of a smile touched Edward's face. "You are my life too, but this is the end."

Richard read the paper over again. "This says that Uncle Richard died at Bosworth Field two years from now." He tried to digest the news and make some sense of it. They were not ghosts; of that he was certain. Nor did this feel like a dream. The wind was on his face. He wiped a tear from his own cheek and tried not to weep for his mother who must be long dead if the notice was true. Edward was the strong one and he could not let his brother lose faith.

Uncle Richard had been re-buried 2015. That was a year ago. He tried to digest that. How could that be true? Maybe it was all a lie, a part of the magic but … if it could be true … How many lives, Kings, wars, dreams and discoveries had gone passed since they were in the field awaiting their fate? He remembered the wizard, the fear, the purple mist and … two figures. Two knights? Two rescuers too late? Or maybe he had dreamed them.

He looked again at the date, then the sky, the wondrous city and some sense told him it was true. Whatever truth was. He knew this was the same place, just in a different time. That had to be magic. What other explanation could there be? Yes, magic had brought them here. Magic had made them history, but now that they had arrived they had moved beyond being history. They were today's new present. Yesterday's now.

Both boys sat on the ground, amazed, silent and totally lost.

∽

Robert was not impressed by the state of the staircase but he climbed to the top floor so that he could get a better view of the area. The city was massive and tightly packed. Many tall buildings coated the horizon. The street below him was fairly busy. He kept in the shadows so that he would not been seen. There was a small gang in the street, loitering not far from the passage which he decided to keep an eye on, but nobody dressed like the 'guards' of the night.

The windows, he noticed, were of a kind of glass more like crystal when cleaned. Most of the buildings had the same kind. He carefully touched and tapped while still trying not to be seen from the road. The walls, too, had a different feel to what he was used to, but they seemed solid enough.

He casually shifted some rubbish on the floor and saw part of a picture. He picked up a page from an old book and dusted it down. It was a picture of a man in green tunic firing an arrow from a bow. The title was 'Robin Hood'. He smiled as he remembered of childhood stories of the old outlaw. This at least was something familiar.

Footsteps brought Ralph into the room, carrying a couple of mugs. He passed one to Robert. "Drink this," he said. "It's called coffee. The old man gave us it." When he saw Robert sniff it and hesitate, he added. "It's safe. It tried it."

Robert took a sip and frowned. "Are you certain?" but he took another sip."

Ralph joined him at the window. "What do you think of Megan?"

"A comely wench," he mused. "But useful if she returns with clothing and coin that can help us in this realm."

He noticed that three of the small gang started heading for the passage while the rest moved away down the street. The knights watched as the three waited until the road was quiet before coming down the passage. They were young men no more than twenty five years in age. It was possible that they were friends of the old man or Megan. Robert drunk more of the coffee. He knew he could get used to the taste.

There were soft voices from the ground floor. Neither knight could quite make out any words. There was a bit of movement followed by a low thud. Robert cautiously crept down the stairs until half way to better judge the events. He could see the old man sitting on a crate. A few words were audible.

One newcomer closed in on the old man who began to cower. The other two began to throw things around the room. Robert stood in the doorway but then lay his mug down on a crate and approached them slowly.

"Who the heck are you?" asked the first man, lightly sneeringly.

"Robert L'aselle," said the knight. "Knight of the realm, defender of the innocent, master of justice, enemy of tyranny, loyal servant of King Edward. Do you want any more?"

The man gave a short snort. "What a toe-rag!"

Robert struck him full in the jaw and knocked him out cold. "I don't actually know what that means but I didn't like the way you said it."

The other two brought out flick knives and circled the knight. Robert was not impressed but experience had trained him to never underestimate his opponent. He also knew that his brother-in-arms was on hand. When the fight began he only had to worry about the one blade. He did not use his own. His chainmail protected him against the first blow and he did not allow his opponent a second chance. Another blow to a jaw and then his enemy was spinning across the room.

Ralph had the other pinned against the wall. "You need to read the field when you go into battle" he told his captive softly. Then he confiscated the knife and threw the man towards the middle of the room. "Pick up your friend and go."

For a second the aggressors hesitated but then decided to limp away to safety. "Pitiful foe!" Robert turned to the old man. "I'm sorry. I assume you wanted them to leave?"

The old man gawped at the knight then found his voice. "Yes. Yes. Thank you. They steal our food."

Sounds of another skirmish were heard and they saw Megan punching one of the young men as they were retreated down the passage. Her words were unfamiliar to the knights but they had no doubt for their meaning.

Robert smiled at Ralph. "I like her spirit," he said.

When in Rome

A young couple were kissing on a bench in Weaver's Fields, a box beside them was playing a song ... *"I poured it on and I poured it out,"* ... and kissing, seemingly without breathing. The boys were seated on a nearby bench; Edward feeling embarrassed and Richard unable to stop gawping. *"I'm crying icicles instead of tears."* ... sung the box.

Several people had passed by but not had paid any attention to the kissing couple or to the boys in ancient costume. It seemed that few things were unacceptable in this strange time or place. Maybe it was a kind of shock that had brought the boys back to the place where they had woken from the dream that had turned out to be more than a strange reality. Even the roaring dragons no longer surprised them; but this kissing was both exciting and unnerving.

"I know you're looking for a ruby in a mountain of rocks," continued the box.

Edward nudged Richard who closed his mouth. A man dressed as an apple paused to look at the boys then smiled and handed them each a piece of paper. It was a colourful flyer but their attention was then diverted to a trio of teenage girls who came and sat down at the end of the row. They wore shorts and crop tops, causing Edward to blush. One was a pale blond; one had red hair and freckles and the other was dark skinned with deep eyes which seemed to probe Edward's soul.

"Hello," said the dark skinned girl. "I love your costumes. They suit you."

Richard's mouth was open again.

"What are your names?"

Edward coughed and found his voice but still tried to avoid eye contact. He had never spoken to a dark girl before and was not sure it was allowed. But then, flying coaches and singing boxes were unknown to him before today. He gave her an unsteady glance. "I'm Edward," he croaked, then cleared his throat. "And this is my brother Richard."

"I'm Amber," she said. "And those are Shelley and Michelle. We are all fourteen. Do you live in London?"

"Yes," said Edward truthfully.

"I wish more boy had the courage to wear long hair and natural like yours," said Amber. "Yours is beautiful! How old are you?"

Edward coughed again. "I'm twelve and Richard is ten."

Shelley, the blond girl, gave Richard's hair a quick stroke. "You're very cute," she told him.

Now he blushed and he looked her over, her slender legs, shapely torso, full lips and tempting eyes. "Are you a whore?" He asked innocently.

She gazed at him open mouthed then giggled. "Oh my god!"

Neither boy really understood girls. Giggly girls were the most difficult to relate to although, so far, life had not given the boys much chance to practice, sisters not included. Richard was quite happy for the girls to gyrate their way to a different part of the park but Edward was torn. He was fascinated by Amber, although he was not sure why.

"Wait," he said. "My brother is young and did not mean to offend. Stay."

"Well," Amber stood in front of him. "As you're such a gentleman, we will stay a while."

"Thankyou."

"Are you always so polite? Or are you in some special medieval mood?"

"Evil?"

"Medieval! As in old." All three girls giggled again.

"Oh, yes." He didn't really understand but thought he had better not seem too ignorant.

"Are you going to the tower or something," she asked, considering his clothes.

Edward noticed that Richard was shooting him a warning look. "What is the better way to get there?" he asked.

She shrugged. "Just get to bus," she pointed to get stop near the gate. "But if you really want to walk just go that way cross the railway and keep going north-ish . It's not far really"

"Thank you."

"No problem," Amber gave him a quick peck on his lips.

What was it that he was feeling? It was not love, not so soon. He tingled. He wanted to kiss her back but … but … her lips were warm and gentle. He pictured her as his queen. There would be much objection but he would be a King who would rise above such things. But he was not King and now never would be. He knew that, deep down, and the whole situation both scared and thrilled him. He could kiss her and not worry about consequences. But …

"Are you ok?" Amber asked him.

He gathered himself. "Yes. Thank you."

She smiled. "You are so-o-o-o sweet! Both of you."

"I'm hungry," announced Richard, to break the spell."

"Oh, you guys want a burger?" asked Amber. "Our treat. Before you go to war, or whatever you're doing at the tower. We'll go to Sam's."

"Is a burger food?" asked Richard.

The girls giggled again. Amber took Edward by the hand and the group headed across the field. Richard declined offers from the other girls to hold hands, even though he felt he was probably being impolite. It was high summer and some boys were playing shirtless in the park. Richard watched them as he walked by, trying to understand the game they were playing. Shelley and Michelle spent most of the short journey tapping on small devices in their hands. There was not much talk.

The streets away from Weavers Fields were buzzing with activity. Shops and a busy open market filled the roadside. Clothing, fruit and veg, jewellery, books and bric-a-brac surrounded the group. Richard automatically held his brother's hand. People passed by them unconcerned. Londoners were too used to the endlessly varying fashions, and customs, of it's inhabitants and visitors. The young group entered a small café and occupied seats at the far side.

Richard wondered at the sounds and smells of this food inn. There was nothing here to make the boys feel awkward or uncomfortable. Amber seemed to have a good relationship with the owner. It was not long before they each had burger and coke before them. Richard tasted the coke and was surprised by the fizzing. "What is it?" he asked suspiciously.

"Coke!" said Michelle simply.

"Haven't you ever had Coke before?" asked Shelley.

"No," said Richard, self-consciously.

"Oh .. my .. god," Shelley half smiled. "You guys aren't from one of them religion nut groups, like the Amish, are you?"

Richard felt himself grow crimson. Edward hung his head awkwardly.

"Don't be daft," said Michelle. "Amish wear big wide hats and beards."

"Boys don't wear beards, silly."

"We are not … that," Edward told her. "We are just … different."

"Do you have TVs and phones and stuff?" asked Amber, hopefully.

Edward looked at her and still felt a buzz when she spoke. He had no problems talking to her and wished he could tell her the while story. "No. I'm not sure what they are," he admitted.

All three girls let their jaws drop dramatically. "You are kidding, yeah," asked Amber but then she read something near panic in Richard's eyes, so she lighted the mood. "Well, who needs stuff like that. Last year I went for a full week camping with any kind of techno. I survived!"

Edward wanted to hug her.

"Oh .. my .. god," gasped Shelley. "I would so freaking die if that happened to me."

"Cos you're a wuss," laughed Amber.

The atmosphere thus relaxed, the group got to work on the burgers. Richard soon had ketchup all over his mouth and a smile on his face. Food can be a tonic. The future was still uncertain for the boys but their immediate present was pleasant.

Suddenly Shelley stood up.

"Selfie!" she shouted, holding her device so that she could capture them all in the pic. She laughed when she checked it back and saw the mess around Richard's mouth. She used a napkin to wipe his face and then .. "Smile guys." She took another couple of pics and showed them. "These are so going on facebook!"

"How does it work?" asked Richard with genuine interest.

Shelley gave him a fun peck on his cheek. "Never you mind," she giggled. "You probably wouldn't be allowed to use one anyway."

He smiled, partly because he now had food inside, and partly because of the kiss. He finished the last dregs of his Coke and then remember another necessity of life. "Do you know what a privy is?" he had to asked.

"Yes," said Michelle. "There's one over there." She pointed to the toilet sign. "Do you guys really call it that?"

"But," added Shelley. "Make sure you get the right door." She giggled again.

"You are too cute," said Michelle, looking at him. "So, you're ten, when's your birthday?"

Richard avoided looking at her and tried to resist his sudden urge to cry. "Today," he said softly.

Shelley beamed. "Oh .. my .. god. That is so cool!"

Amber came across and gave Richard a long hug. He needed the hug so he clung to her for about a minute. She sensed his need but didn't question why. "Happy Birthday," she breathed it more than said it, and he appreciated it.

When he was free from her embrace, Richard made for the doorway. He brushed against a man at the corner table. "I am sorry," he apologized.

"That's ok."

The man seemed to look at him oddly, but Richard guessed it was because of his costume. He saw how Edward was talking freely with Amber at their table and had mixed feeling about that. The man he had brushed against started to speak into one of the devices but Richard thought no more about it. The privy room was small with just sitting down place and a kind of trough and a basin. It smelled odd. Not bad; more like a sweet aftertaste with a hint of lime.

Richard lifted the seat and assumed that the shaft must link to the river. A word on the wall made him blush and he hoped that he would not get the blame for writing it. Ten year olds are ten year olds no matter what the century; if they see something interesting they must test it. There was a button on top of the sitting down place. Richard pressed it and was surprised by the rushing and gurgling of water down the shaft. He backed away as one if the staff came in with spare toilet rolls.

"Did I break it?" asked Richard, watch as the member of staff inspected it.

"I don't think so. Were you trying to break it?"

"No," said Richard, quite defensively."

"Oh .. you're on about the banging sound. Don't worry it does that, it's an old system." He put placed spare rolls in place, fastened a 'Now Wash Your Hands' sign by the sink and left.

Richard looked down the shaft and it was no more flooded than before. *'A privy that cleans itself!'* he muttered. Two more buttons on the top of the wash basin gave water; one making it hot. This was a marvel! He tried another button but it blew hot air on him. He smiled. What other wonders did this new world have?

~

"They feel odd," said Robert, wearing the clothes which Megan had brought. "But if these are the price we have to pay for freedom, so be it." They were casual clothes, cargo trousers, shirt and jacket, and trainers. He looked across at Ralph who wore similar. The several pockets in the cargo trousers were useful for carrying a small dagger if needed.

"Are you sure you need the knives?" asked Megan.

"Yes, we must be armed and ready." He told her.

Ralph looked himself down in the grimy reflection of the window and was not too displeased. "I can live with this," he said. "There is enough room to breathe."

Megan shook a can of scent and sprayed Robert with it. He ducked away and then tried to grab it off her. "What are you doing?" he sniffed and wiped his face. "Am I woman that I should want to smell like that?"

"Don't be a wuss," she said. "Most men use body spray these days. It makes them smell nice and, to be honest, you could do with a shower." She sprayed Ralph also. "But we don't have a shower here so a good dose of this make you more presentable."

"Men should not be ashamed to smell like men," argued Robert.

"When in Rome," quoted Megan.

"Rome?"

"It's a saying." Megan blew a short burst of scent at the old man and then tucked the can among the rags on the floor. "And, despite what you seem to think, we are not at war with anyone right not so no weapons should be needed. I know the police are carrying them more and more but that's a different matter. I gave up expecting anything better from them a long time ago."

"If there has been several years of peace in this land then that is to be celebrated," said Ralph. "How did King Richard die? Was it in battle?"

"What are you on about?" asked Megan, bemused.

"The old man told us about Elizabeth being Queen but we don't know how she became to be so."

Megan gave Ralph a long gaze. "She became so because her father died."

"Her father?" queried Robert.

"King George!" she said. "I take it that neither of you paid much attention in history, though I thought everybody knew that much."

"But what about Richard?" Ralph was feeling more troubled by her words that he expected to be. "Was Richard not King of England before Elizabeth became Queen?"

"The last King Richard was Richard the third and he died hundreds of years ago," said Megan. "But they did just re-bury him last year. Maybe that's what you mean."

"Hundreds of years?" repeated Ralph.

"Do you jest, woman?" asked Robert, quite severely.

Megan sighed lengthily then looked from one knight to the other. "You're both as bad as he is." She motioned to the old man. "Let me update you, ok. We have Elizabeth. Her father was George. His father was also George. Then there was Edward ..."

"Edward!" both knights reacted together. "Which Edward?"

"Seventh, I think. Yes, there was an eighth but he gave it up for a woman so was never crowned." She saw that the knights were looking deeply concerned and no longer particularly listening to her, so she sat down on a crate and lit up a cigarette.

The old man nudged her. "I told you they were interesting," he said.

"Yes," she agreed. "I certainly know how to pick them."

Ralph and Robert went into the yard and looked around, then up at a vapour trail. More than the believed fifty years had passed, that was clear, even to them. The evidence was all around them. Fifty years had become several hundred. Everyone and everything they knew was gone. Family, friends, Adam, their homes; maybe even their purpose in life was obsolete. But if their King Edward and Prince Richard had gone before them into the purple smoke they may still be saveable. No matter how long it takes. Adam's words had new meaning now. No matter at what cost to the knights they had the same duty as always. The same job which still needed to be done.

"We must find out whatever we can about this new England and it's workings," said Ralph.

"Yes," agreed Robert. "I feel we have acted in err already, attacking their law makers."

"A lesson learned, I hope." said Ralph. "We must take heed and do better."

Do better ... but where to begin? We could enquire about local churches but, if no sign of the boys is found, where then? The new England was so strange to them. Ralph looked at the sun and assumed that south was still south. They had been south of the tower then they arrived at this place, but had more than time changed? They could see no familiar point from which to take reference.

"I expect that Megan thinks we are more idiots, like the old man," said Robert.

She was examining the weapons and clothing which the knights had been wearing. The quality of the swords, the stitching in the shirts, the chainmail and everything looked and felt authentic. Too authentic! She smelled the tissue. The old man was watching her with keen enthusiasm.

"What do you think?" he asked her.

She drew on her cigarette and glanced at the knights through the window. "Weirdest kooks I've come across. Even the way they speak."

The old man tittered.

Ralph saw that Megan was looking in his direction and so crossed back into the building to sit beside her. She crushed the cigarette on the floor and waited for him to speak.

"We might seem a bit strange to you," he began

"Hah," she grunted dismissively. "I'm used to that. The world is full of odd people, most of them in high office, so that doesn't bother me." She fingered one of the swords. "These are the genuine article. And the way you both act, and speak, tells me there's more about you than I should reasonably know. Then there's that bit about King Richard. You really aren't from here, are you."

"We are," he said "But, also, it appears we are not."

"Nor was I," chimed the old man somewhat vaguely.

"Ok." Megan let her thoughts rest for a moment and then carried on. "Let's say you've both travelled through time, from the days of King Richard. Why?"

It was a good question. Neither knight had an easy answer so they just told their story as best they could. It sounded quite far-fetched to anyone who had never experienced time travel – which none of them had before today. The knights also included bits of their personal history, battles, family life, etc. Megan listened silently and the old man poured over every word.

"The princes in the tower!" said Megan, suddenly. "But they found two …." She paused and looked at the knights. "Are you sure you saw the boys disappear into the mist. There are one of two tricks that can be done today to make it look like someone has disappeared."

"But we followed them into the mist and we are here," said Robert.

"Why did you pause?" asked Ralph.

"Because," said Megan. "Skeletons of two children were found in the White Tower a couple hundred years later. There have always been questions about whether they were of the two princes. If the boys did travel through time with you then … where are they?"

Robert leant against the wall and grimaced. "That tells us nothing. It takes us no further."

"It's always been supposed that King Richard ordered the deaths," said Megan. "But how much is fact and how much is legend?"

"So, do you believe that our story is true?" asked Ralph.

Megan looked him straight in the eye. "Let's say I'm going along with it for now. There are so many new discoveries. Who's to say that time travel isn't one of those weird things that exist but we are never told about.

They were interrupted by a girl, who seemed barely into her teens, half-cast and wearing a 'Heavy Metal' T-shirt, picking her way through the passage. She stopped at the door, gawped at swords on the floor and the two strangers. "Megan," she called quietly. "Rozzers!"

Megan began to scoop up the weapons and clothing and thrust them to the knights. "Hurry, upstairs. Don't say anything until I give you the ok."

"Kit's holding them up but he'll be here," said the teen.

Megan bundled her and the knights through the doorway but the old man stayed on his crate. Ralph and Robert were used to treading softly and they recognised the urgency in Megan's voice. They placed the clothing behind an upstairs door but kept hold of their swords. The girl hiding with them was a bit alarmed by the weapons. Ralph gave her a quick smile of reassurance.

Voices downstairs. Two men and Megan.

"You need a warrant!" Megan.

"We don't need a warrant in a derelict building!"

"We have permission to be here. Have you?" Megan.

"There were two men here, both in chainmail. I supposed you're going to tell us you didn't see them."

"I saw them. They left after teaching some yobs a lesson." Megan.

"We'd still like to look around."

"I bet you would, but not without a warrant." Megan.

"Maybe we should take you for questioning."

Robert began to move slowly back down the stairs but then handed his sword to Ralph before continuing. He listened at the door for a moment, then flung it open to confront two uniformed police officers. Megan seemed both surprised and annoyed. Robert held a hand to her then faced the officers.

"Good morning," he said, calmly. "Is there a problem?"

"And who might you be?" asked one officer.

"I'm Sir Robert L'aselle," he told them confidently. "I now own this building, and these are my guests."

The officer hesitated before responding. "I wasn't aware that anyone had bought this property. We had reports ..."

"Reports from known troublemakers, I assume," said Robert, sensing that he had the edge. "I advise that you direct your questioning to them."

"May I see some identification please, Sir?"

"No you may not." Robert moved closer to the officer. "I have a busy day ahead. There is nothing to keep you here."

The police officers exchanged glances and backed off slightly. "We have to respond to reports, Sir," said the first officer. "But, as you say, known troublemakers. We'll be sure to have a word with them about wasting police time."

"You do that."

The officers nodded and left. Megan and the old man gazed at Robert. "How on the earth did you do that?" asked Megan. "That first cop can usually be a right pain in the neck."

"They are not confident within themselves," Robert told her. "They may know you but they are not sure about me. They will be back once they have clearer orders. We should not linger about this place."

Ralph and the young girl came back into the main room, she still looking uncertain. Megan said something quietly to her. The girl nodded dumbly and left the building. Ralph brought a wad of notes out from his pocket and studied them. "So this is real currency?" he asked.

"Four hundred pounds," Megan told him. "Your coins were worth money but, like I said, you need to change them quickly so I hardly used a top dealer."

"Four hundred?" asked Robert. "For those?"

"In a reputable auction house you could get several thousand for what you have in your pouch.," Megan told them. "If anyone asks where they came from just say they've been in your family for hundreds of years which, in your case, seems to be true."

"We could get a room in an Inn for these?" asked Ralph.

"You could rent a small flat. It could be your base while you search for the boys."

"We will need your guidance," said Robert. "This place is still strange to us."

"What is a flat?" asked Ralph.

∽

"You kissed her," Richard said bluntly.

"So?"

"On the lips!"

"So?"

"It was disgusting!"

"It was not."

"It's not the thing that a King should do."

"Of course it is," said Edward. "If not, there would be no more princes."

Richard looked his brother in the eye. "I hope you didn't do THAT!"

Edward returned his gaze. "Did it look like I did THAT? You were there. There wasn't time to do THAT."

"How long does it take?"

"I don't know."

"What about the promise you made to Anne of Brittany?" asked Richard.

Edward only hesitated for a moment. "I think she's dead … like everyone else." He considered the implications of that for a while. It was like a heavy weight, far worse than when he heard of his father's death. Worse than his own experience if imprisonment. There had always been hope; rumours of attempts to free him and set right all that had been made wrong. But this was a kind of magic beyond his nightmares. Everything was different now. Amber was a relief from the horror of his fears. Anne had been still a child much younger than he. He hardly knew her. He had certainly never kissed her.

They were back in Weavers Fields again, having said goodbye to the girls. Even now, most people accepted their clothing as just costumes. A reflection of history. There was something reassuring about that but Edward had the feel that it would not last. What about tomorrow, or even tonight? He looked at the number that Amber had written on his hand. He didn't even know what that meant, but he was determined to keep it anyway.

"Are we really going to try to find the tower?" asked Richard, uncertainly.

"Yes, we need to find it so that we can get our bearings in this strange land. Amber said that if we go through the tunnel and keep on going until we reached a stop and then take the right road we shall will get there."

"I don't want to go to the tower," said Richard. "I never want to see that tower again."

Edward put an arm around his brother. "We can't just stay here, and we have no idea how to get anywhere else."

"I know." Fresh tears formed in the younger boy's eyes. He wiped them away annoyingly. "I just want to go home, to mother, to Ludlow. I don't even care that much about being a prince."

Edward understood his feelings. So much had happened the last three months. He had inherited a crown, an army, the countless responsibilities as Head of State, then seen his friends and companions taken away, been labelled as a bastard, locked in the tower, taken out to a field where he supposed he and his brother were to be murdered, then, finally, magicked to this place. His emotions switched from terror to anger, hopelessness to acceptance. They had, indeed, been murdered but also left alive. Sentenced to a kind of living death. If he thought about it too much it would overwhelm him.

"Come on," he urged his brother. "Remember what Sir Ralph taught us. When things look at their worst, we can find new strength within ourselves."

"I wish he was here now," said Richard.

A group of Japanese tourists stopped to point their devises at the boys. One of the men pressed a note into Edward's hand. "Thank you," said the tourist. "Most good. Very good." It was the biggest reaction the boys had known to their costumes. The note said 'Bank of England. TEN Pounds'.

"It must be like a promissory note," said Edward. "At the bottom it says Charles Darwin. I wonder who he is?" The other side of the note showed a picture of a lady wearing a crown. Could it be the new Queen? He wondered what she was like.

"Can we use it to buy food?" asked Richard. "And shelter? How much is ten pounds?"

"I think it's a lot. I heard one of the guards saying that his sword lost nine pennies." He looked around at the city and wondered, again. "But if so much time has passed and some stranger just gave us ten pounds, maybe it is not worth as much now."

"Oh." Richard's hopes faded. "So, we might need more of these?"

"Maybe." Edward glanced up at the sun. "It must be getting near noon. We should make a start." He followed his brother's gaze and saw, sitting a few yards away, the same man they had each seen at the café. He was not looking in their direction. Richard took hold of his brother's hand.

"Are we safe, brother?" he asked. "Are we free from enemies yet?"

"I know not," said Edward. "That man was in the food inn but he might visit this place every day, so far as we know. We must not think the worst, but also we must be careful. We have no escort now."

"Let's leave this place then," said Richard. "Why don't we go back to the church again, to see the priest? Ask his guidance."

"I would not know what to say to him now. So much has changed."

"Now that man is watching us."

"He's not. You just think he is."

"He is. Look."

Edward returned the man's gaze and suddenly felt unsure. Had he followed them from the café? Was he truly watching them, like an agent? Did he know who they were, or was he just showing casual interest? The last few weeks had damaged his trust in people. Were they still under the control of the wizard? The man's gaze continued. Edward tightened his grip on Richard's hand, and they stood up.

"If he follows us, run. He's older so we should be quicker." They began to leave Weavers Field, checking back to see if the man was following them. He was, casually. The boys quickened their pace. The man did too, but still held back enough for it to be not too obvious. The crowd was thicker than the last time they had travelled this stretch of road. Richard held on to his brother as they neared the tunnel. Traffic was loud and overbearing. At the junction they hesitated while men and coaches thronged around them.

The man was still following. Edward wished that they had access to different clothes so that they could be less noticeable. They pressed on, through the traffic to the tunnel mouth. A snake thing was roaring above them. Richard flinched a few times as they dared to enter the echo filled cavern. The man was still with them, watching them. The sped up, through the tunnel, into the grey street beyond. Then they ran.

Many eyes followed the fleeing boys. Edward dragged his brother along a side road where he halted and waited to see if they had lost their pursuer. A group of workmen looked them over and one gave them a wolf-whistle. There was no sign of their stalker. To be sure, Edward led the way through a back alley which seemed to double back to the main street. Here they crouched and rested.

Richard could taste his heart in his mouth. Edward just felt hollow.

"Hey," came a voice from up high. They were both surprised when a dark skinned youth dropped down from a garage top. He was soon joined by three friends. "What are you guys dressed as?"

The brothers stood up as the newcomers surrounded them. Edward held Richard behind him as he faced the leader. "We were just resting. We'll go now."

"Oh no," said the youth. "You don't leave until you pay your due. This is Tigger turf. I'm Tigger. What you got for me? Huh? You got any money in those pretty tights? Huh?" He pushed Edward against the wall.

"Get your hand off me," demand Edward. "Peasant!"

Tigger and his friends laughed. "Peasant? Hah, I love it. This kid cracks me up." He slapped Edward on the cheek. "Naughty, naughty. That's not the way to talk to Tigger. You call me Sir."

"I call you an idiot," said Edward, bitterly. The slap had stolen his dignity, plus it hurt, but he wasn't going to let it show.

Another slap, this time harder. "I only give you a slap because you're so young, but I can whip you vicious if you like. You got to show respect." He began searching through Edwards clothing, pushing the boy against the wall. "You come in my domain with your airs and posh voice like you own the place." He gave Edward a painful dig in the ribs. "Lilly white boy. Call me an idiot, huh!" He rifled through Edward's clothing but found no money. "Disappointing," he said. "Maybe the little one has it the dosh." He hit the little King had and threw him onto the ground.

"You don't know who you're talking to," said Richard, defiantly. "This is Edward, King of England!"

Tigger and his gang laughed more loudly. "King of England? Oh aren't we honoured?" guffawed Tigger. "I love that. The kid's got style." He turned his back on Edward and began frisking Richard. "Money, money, where art thou? You see I know how to talk posh too. Pretty boy! I bet your mummy loves you."

"Don't talk about my mother," sobbed Richard, embarrassed by his tears.

Tigger held the young prince by the jaw and looked him over. "Bet you're a real Mummy's boy. How old are you? Ten? Totally hair less? Maybe we should check."

Edward's vision was spinning but he saw a broom balanced against the garage. He grabbed it; prised the head off it and then tapped Tigger on the head with it. "Get off my brother, you rat faced Moor."

Tigger faced him and Edward stood ready for combat. "You come here, Richard," he called to his brother.

Tigger's gang held on to Richard while their leader sized up Edward. "No, you stay put, Richard," said Tigger. "While I teach your King some manners."

"You're the one who needs manners," said Edward.

Tigger stood tall over the little King and mockingly invited Edward to come at him. "Then I'll teach your brat of a brother. Age don't bother me. No sir. We'll have some fun him. But come on. I was winning fights when I was six, mostly with my old man. So come on, brat."

Edward struck him in the cheek.

"That all you got" asked Tigger, wiping a mark off his face.

Edward swung the broom handle and Tigger skilfully avoided it, but Edward remembered lessons from instructor and followed it up with a knock to Tigger's head. That both surprised and angered the youth so that he came at Edward several times. Each time Edward showed that he was quicker and had better balance. He was not tall but quite lean but he had a good understanding of the art of the staff."

Tigger was visibly shocked by the boy's ability, but he was stubborn and unwilling to lose face in front of his gang. "I'm going to kill you, you hear."

"Not fighting like a pregnant maiden, you won't," Jeered Edward. He ducked an attempt by Tigger, swung the youth over finished with a blow to the midriff which almost laid him out.

"Do you yield?" Edward asked him, standing proudly over his quarry.

Tigger tested his jaw and tasted blood but he was too stubborn to give up. He pushed Edward off him and struggled to his feet. He was embarrassed. Some people had witnessed his humbling from their windows. Even now they were probably enjoying a laugh at his expense. He had to do something to recover his lost reputation. He called two of his gang to stand with him. "Yield? You even use weird words. You think I'd give in to a weasel like you?"

Edward was alarmed. "It is foolish to keep fighting when you don't need to."

"Foolish? You calling me a fool?" Tigger and his two gang members began to circle the little King. "We are going to take you apart. Then we are going to take your brother apart. We are going to enjoy it, and everyone will know that this is still Tigger's turf. You got that? Huh?"

"That's enough," came a new voice.

They each looked around to see man that had been following the boys.

"Bog off you," said Tigger, dismissively. "Go trim your roses or something. This has nothing to do with you."

"Oh, but it has." The newcomer stood next to Edward and gave the boy a reassuring smile. "I am their guardian. If you have a problem then maybe we can talk about it, peacefully."

Tigger sniggered. "Peacefully? Are you joking? I am going to kill these posh rats, and you too, if you want." His expression changed as four of the workman came along the road to stand with the newcomer. Two local men appeared from beyond the garage area where Richard was suddenly dropped by his captor. Tigger considered the situation. "I got more men," he said, backing off. "I got more. I'll be back. You wait. You'll see."

"You're nothing but a cheap punk," said the newcomer. "You need a gang before you can take on a twelve year old boy, and even then you lose."

More people came out from the houses. Tigger glared around, looked as though he was going to say something but the changed his mind. The gang retreated, fading away beyond a playground. Richard quickly ran to hug Edward who dropped his broom handle.

Edward turned to their stalker. "Who are you?"

"A friend!"

"What kind of friend spies and chases?" Edward still had his arms around Richard but his eyes were fixed on the newcomer. "I have known too many friends who turned out to be anything but. I cannot trust anyone sir."

"I understand."

"So who are you? Why did you help us?"

"My name is Alex." He offered his had to Edward but knew it was too soon so he withdrew it again. "We should get off this street and find some place more suitable."

"To do what?" asked Edward, suspiciously.

"So that I can tell you more about who I am, and why I was watching you."

Richard wiped his eyes again and looked Alex over properly. There was something about this man, but he was not sure that. "Where are you from?" asked Richard.

"I live in a part of London called Stepney Green," Alex told them. "If you will allow me I shall take you to my home where you can freshen up and I can tell you more."

"I don't know," said Edward. "We must get to The Tower."

"Why do you want to get to The Tower?" asked Alex. "Is it because you think you might find answers about what has happened to you?"

Edward hung his head. He had no real idea what he might discover at The Tower. "It is no business of yours why we want to go there."

"I don't want to go there," put in Richard.

"Was it at The Tower when time changed?"

Both boys looked at him intensely.

"Or was it at Weavers Fields?" Alex met their look. "That area used to be just swamp and wasteland ... when you were last there!" Alex took a photograph from his pocket and showed it to Richard. The young boy gazed at it and wiped another tear from his eye. He showed it to Edward. "You recognise it?" asked Alex. "It belongs my father. He was given it by you, Richard. I have the actual brooch at home."

"Your father?" asked Richard, confused.

"Miles Griffiths, your loyal servant."

Richard sat down on the kerb and put his head in his hands. "That cannot make sense. How?"

"It's a trick!" suggested Edward.

Alex sat beside them. "Are the flying machines trick? The horseless coaches? This huge city? Is everything you have seen since this morning, a trick?"

"This morning?" asked Edward. "You were watching us all the time?"

"Not all the time. The first time I saw you, your clothing looked authentic, but you were talking with some girls so I wasn't sure. I followed you to the café and then watched you back in Weavers Fields."

"I saw you in the café," said Richard.

"But," started Edward, carefully. "How did you know we would be here?"

"It's a long story," said Alex. "I can't tell you here in the street. Please, come home with me. I can tell you more then."

"Will Miles be there?" asked Richard, hopefully.

Alex hesitated then just said. "My father has been quite ill. He's in hospital."

Richard gazed at Alex. "I saw him just four days ago!"

"I'm sure you did," said Alex. "But that was before I was born. He came here the same way that you did but at a different time." He saw the expressions on the boys faces, part wonder, part horror. "I don't understand how it all happens. Nor does my father. Really, we should move from here."

"How long to your house?" asked Edward, after a moment of reflection.

"Not long. We can get a taxi. A horseless coach." The boys looked doubtful. "They are safe. Please, trust me."

The boys exchanged glances. "Trust must be earned," said Edward. "But we will see how we do together. If you need a pay for the 'tax sea' I have a note." He dug around inside the lining of his tunic and found the ten pound note. "That Tigger did not find it."

"You hold on to that," said Alex. "Keep it for a raining day. By the way, when did you learn to fight like that?"

For a brief moment, Edward hung his head, but then he recovered himself. "My father taught me," he said.

The Need to Know

The flat was in Bethnal Green, not far from Weavers Fields, above a closed pottery shop. It was in budget and belong to a friend of Megan's. Just one bedroom, a kitchen diner and a bathroom. It was only modestly furnished but it served it's purpose. There was no TV or phone but the knights had no idea what such things were. Megan had bought a holdall and a couple of fishing rod cases to help transport the swords and armour. If the police did search the derelict building they would only find dust and whatever rubbish the old man had left.

Electric lights and plumbing were new to the Knights. Robert played with the switches a few times before he was satisfied. Ralph thought the shower was useful; a bit like having a waterfall in the house. Both knights, however, found the task of setting up house frustrating when they thought they should be out searching for their King. In a city which seemed to go on forever, such a mission seemed near impossible, but they each had faced equal odds.

"I'll fetch you a kettle, later," said Megan. "and show you how to make coffee."

"Ah, coffee." Robert even liked the name. "It is one of the good things of this new age."

"Me and the old man will use a squat we know. He'll be safe there until those troublemakers and the police lose interest." Megan sat on a chair arm and hunted in her pocket for her packet of cigarettes. "Milly, the young girl you met earlier, said there's a picture online of you guys, taken from CCTV. Fortunately, it's not a good likeness so they won't be able to identify you. Not that they could do that easily anyway."

"What is CCTV?" asked Ralph.

"It's like having hidden spies everywhere," She told them. "Supposedly, they are for our protection, but I don't believe that. It's policing on the cheap so the rozzers can sit on their bums all day. The good news, though, is that the one you injured is going to be alright."

"That was a misunderstanding," said Ralph.

"We were attempting to free our King," said Robert. "We knew nothing about this change in time."

"Well, what's done is done." She lit up another cigarette. "Do you mind?" she asked, belatedly.

"Why do you do that, anyway?" Robert wafted the smoke away from him. "It cannot be good for you."

Megan smiled, "Honey, you should see me when I don't have any cigs. For me they are a life line." She opened a window and stood by it. "But, you are right, I shouldn't do it in someone else's house."

Robert joined her at the window and looked out. Most of the local traffic seemed to be on foot. A few people had 'cigs' to their lips but just as many did not. The road was quite narrow and, at one end, there was a sorry looking school with walls that carried more graffiti than any other building on the street. Beyond that school, there was a small park.

"No windmills around here," said Megan, more to herself.

"Should there be?" asked Ralph.

Megan shrugged. "You both reminded me of an old story about Don Quixote. He thought he was a knight and he went on a crusade against windmills. He was mad, of course."

Robert looked at her. "You think we are mad?"

She smiled. "I could have done, if not for all the stuff that tells me you're not." She moved away from the window. "Too much seems real, and it's not like you're working for the BBC with all their props. No. Ninety percent of me says you are the real McCoy. The other ten percent I just ignore. So, if your boys are here ... it's a big city ... I think we need to employ Milly and a few of her young friends to use popular media. That's like getting all the updated intelligence. The boys are young, so we use young people to help find them. I assume they'll be wearing clothing from your era."

The knights glanced at each other, a bit mystified.

Megan rolled her eyes. "You know how I said about CCTV is like having spies everywhere? Well, kids are always taking pictures and sharing info on popular media. If Edward and Richard have been out and about, looking totally out of place, it's bound to get noticed and shared."

It seemed like a plan. "So," said Robert. "We are supposed to just sit here and wait? It goes against my nature. Why can we not join this search?"

"Because," said Megan. "You are grown men who will be asking about young boys, with no way of showing how that's any of your business. This is 2016. An age of mass hysteria where all men are assumed to be perverts. Believe me, you do not what to open that can of worms. It's worse than the old witch hunts of the sixteen hundreds ... which you also won't know about. It's humanity. Every few decades we seem to be programmed to lose whatever common sense we were born with." She took a long drag on a cigarette. "Anyway, it's just better left to the kids."

Ralph digested her words for a moment. "Your world is no better than ours," he said. "Just different."

"Apart from the coffee," suggested Robert, with a half smile.

The old man came out of the bedroom. "I fell asleep," he admitted. "And I dreamed like I have not dreamed for a long time. Not since ..." He sat on a chair and tried to remember something lost in the archives of his soul.

Ralph patted the old man's shoulder. "Worry not, old man. It is a strange age for all of us."

The old man huffed as an image formed in his mind. "I had a slingshot," he said, triumphantly. "A slingshot and a bag of rocks ... or were they marbles?"

"And then you lost yours," suggested Megan. She looked at the knights. "For all I know he could be from the same time as you, the amount of sense he makes."

"Why do you stay with him?" asked Robert.

"Who else would look out from him?" asked Megan. "She's not bad company, not really. There are worse people I could spend time with." She watched the old man for a few moments, as he tried more of his hidden history. "In our own ways, we are both odd bods."

There was a knock on the door. Ralph opened it to allow Milly to come in. The girl still seemed a bit unsure about the knights, edging around them to sit with Megan. By the cleaner light of the mid afternoon sun they could see that she was surprisingly attractive and maybe part Moor. On the streets they had seen many people of Moorish appearance but the days of the Crusades were well past, even for the English knights.

"Have you got something already?" Megan asked Milly.

The girl tapped a few times on her tablet and scrolled down to a post on Facebook. "This was just posted this morning. I don't know the girls but it's from around here, Sam's Café. Is this the boys you are looking for?" She showed the screen to the knights.

"Tis Edward and Richard!" exclaimed Ralph. "God be praised."

"Where do we find them?" asked Robert.

"I doubt they'll be there now," said Milly. "But there's five of us looking around so, unless they've changed, we should see them."

"I don't think they will have changed," said Ralph.

Megan looked at him. "Why not? You have."

"Sausages!" muttered the old man.

Megan gave him a quick glance, then looked at the picture again. "It doesn't look like they are in any kind of trouble, tucking into burgers and talking to girls."

"Edward is a natural diplomat," said Robert, simply.

"Oh, that's what you call it?" she smiled Softly.

Robert met her gaze. "Indeed!"

Milly tapped on her tablet and then tucked in her bag. "I've sent a copy to all the gang. All we can hope is that one of us gets more info." She saw that Ralph was looking at her. "You don't want them for anything bad, do you?" she asked him.

"No," he assured her. "Nothing bad. They've been lost and had a terrible time. We are trying to take them home."

Megan put an arm around Milly. "Do you think I'd be mixed up with anything bad?

The girl shook her head. "No."

"Well then. We could all do with some food, and Ralph seems to be in the money, so why don't we go by Sam's Café. Even if the boys are not there, it's a starting place. Who knows what we might find out in the process. You come too, Milly. We need your teen input."

⁂

"Bring it out?" said Edward. "We shall wait out here until we see it."

Alex turned the key and went into the house, but he left the door open so that the boys could see what kind of place it was. It was well made, had three floors plus a basement. Steps led up to a blue front door and there were two windows on each floor. Edward backed off to get a better look. It was not a peasant's house, nor a servant's. Maybe Miles only worked for the master.

It was quite an experience, driving in the taxi, seeing all the tall buildings of the city. One impressive building seemed to be made of pure glass. Not even the grandest castles could match what the boys saw in this new London. Opposite the house, which was part of a string of similar houses, there was a small tree lined garden protected by metal railings. Edward blink several times in the sunlight.

Alex returned and handed the brooch to Richard who sniffed it, kissed it and held it close to his heart. "It is the same one I gave to Miles!" He let Edward examine it.

"Now," said Alex. "Come in and see your house?"

"Our house?" asked Edward.

"Come in." Alex held the door open for them. They stepped in. At first warily, but then with resolve. It was neat and clean but obviously lived in. A photo on the sideboard caught Richard's attention. An elderly man posing with a dog. The man was Miles, but much older than the boys had seen him before. Richard picked up the photo and brushed a tear from his eye. He sat down on the sofa; the most comfortable seat he had ever sat on.

Culture shock can take a while to adjust. The boys tried to take it all in, paintings, ornaments, furniture, the carpet. Maybe this was Heaven after all. But ... Edward could still feel the bruises from his fight. That had not been heaven. He wondered what the rest of the house was like. "How many people live in this house?" he asked.

"Just my father, most of the time," Alex told him. "I have a house in York, but I visit here a lot and have a room which I use as my own. Oh, and there is Arthur of course."

"Who's Arthur?"

Alex opened another door beyond and allowed a border collie dog come in. "This is Arthur, as in the picture."

Arthur wagged his tail, crossing from one boy the other. "Why does he not bark?" asked Richard, giving the dog a huge hug.

"Arthur only barks at people he doesn't like."

Both boys enjoyed the canine company, and Arthur obviously liked them. It was a good ice breaker. The dog sniffed them each several times, noting the unfamiliar but interesting smell from another era. Richard climbed onto the floor with Arthur and was soon relaxed. He had loved his own dog. Arthur was a reminder but also a treasure.

Edward smiled at the sight. He gave Alex a nod. "How could Miles come by such a house?"

Alex sat on a chair opposite him. "Well ... you might know that my father was quite a gambler. He liked to play games. When he was first in this time he had nothing but his wits, so he used the best talent he had, and was successful."

"He made me a promise that he would never play games like that again," said Edward.

"When you find yourself down you do whatever you can to make sure you're not out," said Alex. "And he wanted to provide for the chance that you might follow him to this time. This house is yours once you reach the age of eighteen, and yours to call home for now and for as long as you want."

Edward took another look around the room. "But how could he be sure that something would happen, like has happened? He is just a servant. I do not believe he was a wizard."

"He was a servant who had been sent forward in time." Alex paused. He had imagined this moment so often but was still surprised it was actually happening. "He believed you would come, but he did not know when. Not exactly when, anyway. He knew you had disappeared around the time of Richard's tenth birthday. All he could hope for was that you survived and that you would arrive in the same place, which is now Weavers Fields. He bought this house and furnished two rooms to suit both of you."

"How was he sent forward in time?" asked Edward. "Was it a wizard?"

"He was part of a plot to free you and restore you to the throne, but he was discovered. Someone reported the plot and those involved were arrested. My father was taken prisoner. They took him with three others to what is now called Weavers Fields, and some kind of ritual took place."

"With hoods and purple mist," said Edward, with full understanding.

Richard stopped playing and now listened, still on the floor. "How did he know it happened on my birthday?"

"It might be a lot to take in just now."

"No." Edward said, solemnly. "We need to know."

Alex took a folder from a drawer on the sideboard. He sorted a few papers. "To us it's all history." He handed a printed page to Edward. "You, Edward, are officially known, in history, as King Edward the fifth, even though you were never crowned."

Edward felt a tug on his heart, as though the whole of history had come upon him. There was a painting of him as Prince of Wales, which he recognised. A chart showed how Edward fitted in between his father and his uncle.

"This next painting is of what one artist thought you both looked like as the Princes in the Tower. That's how you are remembered, because you disappeared one day. It's a famous mystery." He gave them time to reflect on that painting, wondering what must be going through their minds." He noticed how Richard turned away first.

"Just disappeared," echoed Edward, hollowly.

"Most people blamed your uncle," said Alex. "But nobody could prove anything."

"What do people say about us?" asked Edward, a bit hesitantly.

"Mostly good," he said. "People were on your side. They wrote stories and poems about you."

"I wish more people had come forward when we needed them," said Edward, though not as bitterly as Alex had expected. He stared at Alex and knew there was more. "Tell me." he said simply.

Alex knew they had to be told at some point. "The skeletons of two children buried in the walls of The White Tower, about two hundred years later. It was believed that they were you, but it was never properly tested." He felt mostly for Richard who was looking totally horrified. "The skeletons were placed in a tomb in Westminster Abbey."

"A Royal Tomb?" asked Edward.

"It's not us!" cried Richard. "It's not!"

Alex brought a box of tissues out from a drawer and gave the younger boy some in his hand. Richard guessed what they were for and so dabbed his face. "What happened to our mother?" asked Richard.

Alex suspected that the boys would benefit from a break before he told them more, so he made the story brief. "Your mother lived on and made arrangements for sister, Elizabeth, to marry Henry Tudor. You said you know that your uncle was killed in battle. That battle was against Henry Tudor, so your mother played a major part in your uncle's demise. Your sister's children, your nephews and nieces, went on the mould the future of this country."

Richard was weeping against Arthur's warm body. Edward remained silent for a while, ingesting the details. He wiped his own eyes and was quite flushed with emotion. Alex put the papers back into the folder and put that back in the sideboard. "So, mother helped unite the nation?" asked Edward.

"She must have been a resourceful woman."

"Yes." Edward wiped his eyes again. "Can we ever get back? Ever?"

"I don't even know how you or my father came to be here in the first place. I mean, what power was used."

Edward said nothing more for a while, just sat with his head in his hands. Eventually, Richard climbed up to sit with him while Alex left them with their thoughts. This was their private moment. He went into the kitchen and switched the kettle on. The day had been weird enough for him. He could only imagine how it had been for the boys. Their world had been totally ripped apart.

A watched kettle never boils. Time seemed to have stopped as he leaned against the worktop, tapping a teaspoon on his chest. What if the boys could not ever get back? His father seemed to have assumed that they never will; or was he just being his normal careful self, planning for every eventuality? But here he was with two preteen boys in his charge. Two boys who did not officially exist. Two boys from the mists of time. If they could not get back to their own time, what should be the next step. All he could do was take each day as it comes.

The kettle did boil. He went through the routine of making tea without thinking too much about it. A bird fluttered against the window, then Alex saw Edward, red eyed but determined, glancing around the kitchen and then looking directly at him.

"When can we see Miles?" he asked.

"Do you think you're able to cope with yet more stuff today?" asked Alex.

"Yes. We must." Edward hung his head slightly. "He's all we have left."

Alex was tempted to put a comforting hand on the little King, but resisted. It was the last thing that Edward would want, he thought. Best not to threaten his dignity. "We cannot visit him until after six tonight." He focused on a small tear in Edward's tunic, and a few smudges in his face. "You need to clean up first."

Edward saw himself reflected in the shine on cupboards. He felt suddenly awkward. He was an orphan, poor, lost in a strange place. He wanted to yell at the world but, instead, he looked at Alex, and remembered Amber. Soon he would see Miles. He and Richard were not alone in this strangeness. "I have nothing else to wear."

Now, Alex put a gentle hand on the boy. "You have more that you think."

The little King looked at the hand, felt it and accepted it along with Alex's friendship.

Alex led both of them upstairs. The house still seemed grand to the boys, but so did the rest of what they had seen of London. The first room they entered was a library. Edward was an avid reader but he wondered if he would ever finish some many book as he tried to count them. He picked one up. 'The Ghost of Grey Minster'. The printing, and some of the spelling, was not too difficult to adjust to. Then he saw 'The Canterbury Tales' on the table. "I read this one with Miles," he remembered.

The next room was designed for Richard. There was a map of the word on the wall opposite the bed, and a spinning globe on a desk. Several figurines of knights on a shelf, and a model of a ship on the window ledge. Alex opened the wardrobe and a chest of drawers so that Richard could see the choice of clothing.

"All for me?" he asked, amazed.

The next room was for Edward. He stood in the doorway to get the full picture. Similar to Richard's but with a poster of all the Kings and Queens of England (including himself). A telescope by the window. A small bookcase. A desk with writing set and calendar. Miniature castles on a shelf, and a replica sword and shield above the bed. He also had a large choice of clothing.

"Miles has been a good servant!" He thought moment and then changed his wording. "He is a good friend!" He tested the bed and then looked out of the window.

"The bathroom is next to yours," Alex told him. "The privy. Have you seen modern day bathroom yet?"

"I have," said Richard, appearing at the door with one of his figurines.

"The style of clothing has changed, as you have seen," Alex told them. "It might feel strange at first, but I'm sure you'll get used to it." He saw the number on Edward's hand. "I take it that's the number of one of the girls you were with."

"Amber," said Edward.

Alex showed him an address book on the desk. "Write it in here, so you don't lose it" he said. "You see, there's a section for each letter of the alphabet." He demonstrated the ballpoint pen also.

"I don't know what the number means," admitted Edward.

"It's a phone number," said Alex. "I'll show you how to use it later, Ok. I'll leave you to get settled. I'll just be downstairs."

The boys watched him go out then sat holding hands on the bed. "Are we safe now?" asked Richard.

Edward considered the brightness of the room and the fact that Alex had left the door ajar. He saw that the key was in the lock. He took it out and tested the weight, then placed it on the inside. He locked it, then unlocked it again, then opened the door and left it ajar again. It felt good to have that power over his freedom again. "I think so," he said, with a relaxed sigh.

∽

"The coffee was different!" remarked Robert. "I wonder how many different tastes of coffee there are in this new world."

"You have coffee on your brain," said Ralph.

"It sharpens the mind." Robert scanned the windows of the nearby shops. "We must buy some to keep us alert for our quest."

Megan smiled at his simplicity. "You are becoming an addict."

"A what?"

"It means you can't live without it. You're hooked, and it's only been a day."

They were entering Weavers Fields by the north gate. Milly had discovered from the staff at Sam's café that the boys and their girl-friends had left quite a while ago. No surprise there. It was a possibility that they had gone to Weavers Fields because one of the girls, Michelle, lived just beyond the park. It was a warm day so the park was quite packed. The knights did not recognise it in the daylight until they saw the building that they had thought was a wizard's manor.

A frisby whizzed by and Robert caught it instinctively. A young boy came running up. Robert looked down on him and then examined the frisby. "What was your purpose in throwing that at us?"

The boy boldly looked up at the knight. "Give it back, you nutter."

Megan took the frisby off Robert and handed it back to the boy who sped away to join his friends. "It's a game," said Megan. "That was just a child. This is the twenty third century, remember. People do not attack others ... not like that anyway."

"It looked quite lethal."

"It's just flimsy plastic."

Robert gave a final glance at the boy and then dismissed the incident. He saw that Milly was edging away from him. "There is nothing to fear from me," he assured her.

"I hope not," she said.

"I am just not used to 'frisbys'. I shall know better next time."

"That was quite a catch you made," she said. "You should have gone in the Olympics."

"I do not know Olympics, but if I did, maybe I would."

"The Olympics, like it's on all day on TV." She searched his face for any indication he knew what she was talking about. "In Rio?"

"I must have missed that."

She thought she caught a slight hint that he was teasing her, but he also seemed quite genuine, so she dropped the subject. How old was he? About thirty, maybe? And the other one ... both strange, but kinda nice too. She suspected that they could be quite scary if they were not on her side. Actually, they were scary anyway. "Have you ever killed anyone?" she asked suddenly. She had not meant to ask it out loud.

"Why do you ask?"

"It don't matter," she said, wanting to know more about him, but not wanting to know. He was tall and strong. She checked herself. Did she fancy him? No. That was not it, but he was solid and, she thought, dependable. So was the other one. She glanced Ralph who, she thought, had friendly eyes. She was glad the knights were on their side ... if there had to be sides.

This looked like the place where they had seen the fox. The knights felt nothing. There seemed to be no magic in this place. Maybe the magic only worked at night, or when the wizard was nearby. Ralph thought back to the moment when they had entered the purple mist. The wizard had vanished, they thought. What if he had just hidden behind the mist, somehow? If so, where did that leave them and the boys. Was there any way back?

The old man was staring at the ground, thinking deeply. He sat on the grass and began to mutter to himself. "Something about the night," he mused. "A secret night. Long long ago. Right here!"

The knights looked at Megan. "What's he talking about?" asked Ralph.

"Nothing much," she said. "He's said stuff like this before. It never seems to mean anything. His mind is so muddled from all the rubbish they poured into him over the years."

"Mayhap." Ralph crouched bedside beside the old man. "A secret, long ago. The night. Maybe we just need to put the pieces in the right places."

"What's going on?" asked Milly.

"I'm not sure," admitted Megan. "This beats me."

Ralph looked at the old man in the eyes. "You said something about the others. They found the others. Who were the others?"

"I don't remember," said the old man. "It was all so long ago."

"Have you seen us before?" Ralph pointed to himself and Robert.

"Yes, in my shack!"

"People like us, in this place, with clothes like the ones we were wearing."

"Here," the old man muttered. "Always here ... until you came ... but that not so long ago."

"Always here," echoed Robert. "That might fit in with our story."

Megan was still not sure. "Or it could just be more ravings."

Milly's tablet beeped in her bag. She stood away from the rest and was in conversation with someone. The old man fell asleep again so Ralph let him doze. He was certain that the old man's words had some reason. Had the old man been another victim of the wizard? If so, why? Who was the old man, and how did he fit into the main picture ... if he did?

Milly had made more progress. She was on the phone with one of her contacts. Someone she knew, knew someone who was a friend of someone who knew Amber. They thought Amber lived around Mile End, near the hospital. "She's getting back to me," she told them.

The old man grunted and woke up again. He didn't understand where he was, until he realised he was sitting on grass. "Hmm," he muttered. "Yes. That was the place. That rock. I got a big bump from that rock. I should have thrown it at him."

The rock was deeply embedded in the ground, almost invisible. "Was this rock here, so long ago?"

The old man looked at him vacantly. "What rock?" he asked.

∽

"You still smell!" said Edward, looking at Richard.

"I didn't know it was going to shoot out like that!"

The boys had chosen modern clothes from their rooms. Sweatshirts, jeans and slip on shoes. They had managed fairly well in the bathroom but Richard had tried a spray scent and now reeked of it. He went back to change. Found a colourful t-shirt and returned it wearing it. "Is it alright to show my arms? I saw other boys wearing these."

Alex looked them both over. "Yes. Each of you could use more sun."

The boys were quite enlivened by the prospect of seeing Miles. There was no need to use a taxi this time because the hospital was just a short walk away. To anyone who did not know Edward and Richard, they were just like any normal kids. A bit off key in the fashion sense, but not so much that they would stand out.

"At the hospital, or anywhere else outside of here, you are both my nephews," Alex told them. "It's just in case anyone asks."

They both nodded. "We understand white lies," said Edward. "They are sometimes necessary." He watched Alex lock the front.

This part of the city did not seem so packed as others had, apart from the cars and buses. Neither boy knew why the horseless coaches were called that, but they accepted it. They had noticed, in most places in this new world, that people hardly talked to each other. It was like a city of strangers, in many ways. There was something called a 'retail park' just off their road. A host of impressive buildings lined the way to the hospital. The only really scary but interesting part, for the boys, was when they had to cross main junction, but they crossed that obstacle without too much fuss.

"What it that?" asked Richard, pointing ahead to a distant, tall, curiously shaped building.

"It's called The Gherkin." Alex frowned at it. "I'm not sure who's idea it was. They were probably drunk. It's a bit of an eyesore."

Edward read the large lettering at the top of a building they were passing. 'The Royal London Hospital'. "Is this where we were going? It's Royal?"

"Yes, the entrance is just along here." Alex led the way.

"It's big!" observed Richard.

"It's a big city," said Alex.

Inside, the boys felt their stomachs lurch as they experienced an elevator for the first time. It was quick, but surprising, and left them wondering what had happened. When the door opened again they sprung out and backed away from it. Alex laughed at their expressions and gave them a moment to recover.

"What was that?" asked Edward.

"It's ok, it's safe," said Alex. "It's just a quick way to go from one floor to the other."

"You could have warned us," said Edward.

Richard swallowed and checked himself, then he looked at Alex. "Can we do that again?"

Alex ruffled the boy's hair, pleased to see him smile. "You go sit in those chairs while I go and prepare my father for the news. He's waited a long time for this day. I won't be long. I promise."

Edward watched him leave and sniffed at the odd smell of the hospital. It was different to the smell of Richard's scent. An old woman slowly went by, using a kind of frame to balance herself. A few people used the elevator. A woman in a uniform winked at Richard as she came out from the ward. Seconds became minutes. Edward browsed a magazine, then Alex appeared and beckoned them to come in.

Miles looked tired but elated to see them. They studied him for a short moment but then, completely certain that it was indeed their beloved servant, they rushed to him and hugged him. There were no words for a while. Alex allowed them space. Richard was tearful, again, but more of joy than sorrow. Edward was more composed, holding one of Miles' hands.

"I knew you would come, some time," Miles said, looking at each in turn. "In my heart I knew that the bodies they found could not be you."

Edward considered the lines in his old servant's face. "I am sorry you are not well" he said.

"I feel much stronger for seeing you," said Miles.

"Did they hurt you much," asked Edward. "When they arrested you. I know you were trying to help us. You have been a good, faithful friend."

"There were three of us sent into the mist," recalled Miles. "I lost touch with the others after a few years. They might be dead by now. That was over forty years ago. I never moved far from this place; not once I read about your disappearance. I knew, then, that there was a chance so, each year around this time I keep a watch for you. This year I had to leave that to Alex, my son, who I know will take good care of you while I cannot."

"I like my room!" Richard told him. "And Arthur." He was resting his head on Miles' lap.

"I know it must have been a terrible experience for you both," Miles kissed Richard's knuckle. "The man who did this must be stopped, but I cannot think how. I have pondered on that since that day." He looked Edward in his eyes. "But I knew you would be strong. You would come through it all like a true King should."

Edward hugged him. "If you had not been here ..."

"But I am ... and Alex is."

"Yes." Edward gave Alex a thankful nod. "But I am no King now."

"Being a King is not just about your position in life," Miles told him. "It's about how you face life. How you conduct yourself. It's about knowing what is right and staying true to that. Your father knew that. He was a good King, and he was proud of you because he knew would be a good man. It's not about having a crown, but having a good heart."

Edward wiped his eyes and nodded understanding. "I hope I can be a good man."

Miles kissed him. "You already are, and you will always be my King."

Edward looked at the various symbols, signs and equipment around the hospital bed. He considered the way Miles had aged. The impossible had happened, in ways he could never have imagined. "We are not going to get back are we."

"I don't know how," said Miles truthfully. "But I love you both and you are not alone. Stay strong."

Richard pressed his hand. "Get well, Miles. We need you."

"I have no intention of going anywhere soon," said Miles. "Apart from back home, to be with you again."

"Mother is dead!" Richard kept his head down as he admitted it.

"Yes, my child, but you will always have her love."

"I shall never cry again," said Richard.

"Yes you will," Miles told him. "You must, and you should never be ashamed about it."

Emotion's Eve

Ralph and Robert retreated to their own designated territory to rethink. Megan had agreed to meet them once she'd got the old man settled in the squat. Milly was going to contact Megan after she'd got a call from her own contact regarding the girls who had met Edward and Richard. They had an hour to kill, so they decided explore the local tavern. The name above the door read 'The Royal Oak', which they thought was a good sign.

It was quite busy but they found an empty table by the window. There was subtle music in the background. People were chatting over it. Neither of the knights knew the current custom was so they waited for a moment and the Ralph decided to go to the bar to get some service. Megan had given them some pointers on prices and the new money, so now was a chance for him to see how he managed.

A youngish man came along and greeted him. "Hi, I'm Mark. What can I get you?"

"Two ales, please." said Ralph, simply.

"Which brand?" asked Mark

"Ah," Ralph had not expected a choice. "What do you recommend?"

Mark shrugged. "I quite like Kentish."

"Then, two Kentish ales." Ralph looked around for list of prices like he had seen at the café, but could not find one. A man was eating chips at a nearby table. They looked good so he asked what they were.

"Chips," said Mark. "Just regular chips."

"Could I get two portions of those too?" Ralph took a chance on a twenty pound note.

"I'll bring them across for you," said Mark, checking the note in the light and dealing the change from the till.

"Thankyou." That seemed to go well, thought Ralph, pleased with himself. He returned to the table and examined the few small sachets.

"Almost everyone we have seen today has a thing they mutter into," said Robert, uncomfortably. "Even the maiden Milly. I don't like it."

"Megan told us they are things people use to talk between distances."

"Why would they want such things?"

"I think I just answered that." Ralph winked on him.

Mark arrived with the drinks. "Chips will be here shortly."

Robert studied his bottle. "Kentish?" He took a swig and tested it in his mouth. "Not bad! What are chips?"

"Not sure," admitted Ralph. "Some kind of food."

Robert watched the people parading past the window, young and old, different colours, different shapes. It had only been a day since they had arrived in 2016, but it seemed like an eternity. He barely noticed the feel of his modern day clothing now. Was he changing despite himself? All of his dreams and memories were intact, for now. The only thing that gave him comfort was the fact that they had made some progress in their quest to find their King.

Mark brought their chips. Roasted potatoes! They were very good.

"I still think the old man knows much," said Ralph. "Deep in that mad head of his. I am happy that our King and Prince Richard have made friend of this girls, that eases my mind somewhat but, if there is no more progress by tomorrow, I say we bring the old man to our rooms and see if we can work out his secrets."

"Indeed," agreed Robert. "If he knows anything, we shall have it out of him."

"He seems to be at his best when he had been asleep," said Ralph. "If we watch him and take note of what he says when he first wakes up, we might learn much more about him."

"It is possible," said Robert, glancing out the window again. "That we are within a short walk of our King but do not know it. This city is so vast. Do you think the rest of the country is likewise?"

"If they have ceased warring and have advanced against illness, that might account for so many people." Ralph suggested. "The number of Moors we see in these streets might mean that all wall is at end."

"I think not," said Robert. "At the café I heard news of a war in the east. Maybe another crusade. There have always been people from other lands in this city; merchants and sailors and such. Maybe they settled here are bred over the years."

Ralph agreed the point. He finished his final chip and relaxed in the chair. "But this is not a bad time, compared to our own. The air is clearer, even in the privies."

"But it is not home," said Robert. "I prefer the open highway and my trusted steed, not these carts without horses. But … then there is coffee."

Both knights smiled.

The familiar figure of Megan came into sight from across the road. They watched her approach and then Ralph signalled to her through the window. She came in boldly in her usual manner and sat with them. "What news?" asked Robert.

"Nothing startling," she told him. "Milly did hear from Amber, via another contact, and they plan to meet tomorrow. There is nothing we can do until then."

"More waiting," grunted Robert.

"Patience my friend," said Ralph. "Maybe fate will be kind to you and give you some villains to assault, though this tavern seems peaceful enough."

Robert just gave him a look.

Megan nudged Ralph. "Are you going to buy me a drink, or what?"

"What does a lady drink in this age?" he asked.

"Anything she wants, but I'll have a martini, as you're in the money." She smiled at him.

"Martini." Ralph memorised that and returned to the bar.

Megan let her eyes scan Robert. She started at his feet, paused at his torso and broad shoulders, then moved up to his neck. He was the sort of man than most women would linger over. She knew he was aware of her attention. "This will be your first night in the twenty first century. Is there anyone back home who will particularly miss you? A wife, perhaps."

"There is not," he said simply.

"No female companion?" she probed.

"No." He met her gaze. "I am a knight, swore to honour. My life is not merely about fighting wars. I must meet the standards that are set for me."

"And I'm sure you do, but you are also a human being. We all have needs."

"Indeed," he agreed. "But I do not let them detract me from my duty of honour. If you are trying to tempt me mid quest, you shall fail."

She shrugged and smiled. "You're quite a man but, no, I'm not after your body. I'm just making conversation, and your quest, as you call it, is on hold until we find your little King."

"I am not unduly worried about Edward," said Robert. "He is tougher than he might appear, and he can be artful. He has been ruler of Wales since infancy. If it is God's will that we get back to our own time, I shall serve him as my King."

"And die for him?" she asked.

"Indeed."

Ralph was still getting the Megan's martini from the bar. She watched him for a few seconds than asked. "Has Ralph got anyone special, or is he young free and single like you?"

"Ralph's betrothed died of the fever about a year ago," said Robert. "It's best not to ask him about that."

The knight in question returned and handed Megan her drink. She sucked on the olive and then put it on the side while she enjoyed her drink. Ralph examined the coins in his pocket, noting the changing imagines of The Queen. He showed a fifty pence piece to Robert.

A couple of boys were talking along the street. They paused opposite the pub, wearing casual 2016 fashion gear. The eldest had blonde hair not unlike Edward, but they were too at ease. The younger of the two looked across at the pub and seemed to meet Ralph's eyes for a moment. Then a woman, possibly their mother, joined them and they walked on towards the park.

"I hope the King and prince Richard are in good hands," said Ralph. "I feel like I am letting them down by just sitting here."

"What else could you do, until morning?" asked Megan.

"In just two days more we could have had a force of six hundred men to take the castle by night," said Ralph. "We had agents within the walls to help prepare the ground. We were so close to freeing the rightful King, with his uncle away in middle England, the time was ripe. Just two days and all this could have been avoided. We were betrayed!"

"The King was betrayed," said Robert. "As were all the right thinking people of England."

Ralph leaned closer to Megan and checked to see if nearby revellers were listening. "What is this new Queen like? Would she be willing to grant us an audience? Could we plead our case to her, if the next day doesn't present us with the fortune that we need?"

Megan finished her drink and then looked at Ralph with a mixture of compassion and pity. "You are joking, aren't you? You might be knights in your own century but, here and now, you are just a couple of guys who nobody has ever heard of."

"Knights of England," said Robert. "Are knights until the day they die."

"But you are not expected to still be alive after five hundred odd years," Megan told him. "You are well out of time in that sense." Her mobile beeped and she answered it. "Hmm ... Ah yes ... We could ... Really, that's quite interesting ... At the Royal Oak, yes ... Yes, see you in a bit."

"I was not aware you had one of those things." Robert told her.

"It's Milly's old one," she said. "I don't normally carry one." She put it in her pocket. "That was Milly, she's coming out to meet us in a while. There is someone she wants you to meet."

"I'm still amazed that you can talk to people from a long distance on those things." said Ralph.

"I still do not like them," said Robert.

Somewhere outside, a clock chimed the hour, possibly at St. Dunstan's but Alex couldn't remember whether that clock had a chime or not. The television was showing Olympics coverage. Alex had it turned low but he was also re-reading his father's notes about the boys. The road outside was quiet. Only a solitary woman, wearing a half burka, lingered passed the house. The window was open but the warm, close, air would not refresh. No breeze even dusted the lace curtains.

Alex took a sip of iced ginger ale and noticed Edward in the doorway. The boy was wearing shorts under a loose blue karate style dressing gown. He staring at the television, but more in interest than horror. "I don't think you're a wizard," he said to Alex. "So what makes the paintings move?"

"It's called TV," Alex explained. "It's powered by lightning, sort of, like the lamps and many other inventions you have seen today. It's not magic."

Edward kept his eyes on the screen while he sat down on the sofa. "There are many things which I found scary this morning but now I find less so."

"I see you've selected something cool from your wardrobe."

"Yes. Miles often helped me choose my dress for the day." Edward inspected his naked chest and found a dark bruise which had developed since his fight with Tiger. "It is very warm tonight. I was glad to find something thin that would let me breathe. My brother has fallen asleep on his bed with Arthur beside him."

"You must be tired yourself," said Alex. "You've had quite a day."

Edward sat back in the sofa and enjoyed the softness, but he was still troubled. He watched the activities in the TV screen without actually watching them. Yes, it had been quite a day. Where it ranked among all the other significant and unforgettable days since his father had died, he was not sure. He turned his head and tried to read the notes in Alex's hand; then thought he was being too nosey, even for a King.

Alex noticed his interest. "Do you remember someone called Dominic Mancin?" he asked.

"Yes. I met him when he and my father visited Ludlow."

"You seem to have made a good impression," said Alex. "He wrote this about you *'He had such dignity in his whole person, and in his face such charm, that however much they might gaze, he never wearied the eyes of beholders'*. I guess that means he thought you were good looking ... which you are."

Edward only half blushed. "He was kind to me." He hung his head slightly but then looked at Alex. "Thank you for all that you have done for me and Richard."

Alex put his notes aside and rested down in his chair. "It's been a pleasure ... and an honour, to have you enter into my life," he told the boy. "Even though you are not my King, you are very special."

Edward pondered the words. "I am not anyone's King now."

"You are my father's King, and always will be."

Edward closed his eyes and sighed. "I am so tired, Alex. All I want to do is sleep, but I am afraid. For the last few days every time I sleep I have been tormented by the most terrible nightmare. Now, I am in a different time, with different people. Everything is different. Now ... if I sleep, will I wake to see the walls of the tower again? Or will you be here? Or will things be even more different?" He swallowed and wiped a tear from his cheek. "I am so, so very tired!"

Alex transferred to the sofa and sat beside the boy. He put one arm around Edward. "Nobody should have to go through what you went through, especially someone so young. But, I shall be here. I'm not going anywhere."

"I hope," breathed Edward.

"I promise!"

The boy rested against the man. "Why has this happened to us? I mean, why did they not just kill us?"

"Don't even think about that right now."

"It's not so easy."

Alex placed a fatherly kiss on the top of Edward's head. "How about some hot milk? It sometimes helps he to sleep."

"You mean like straight from a cow?"

Alex laughed. "No, I mean boiled milk. Maybe with a sprinkle of sugar." He led the boy into the kitchen and filled a small pan. "Some people use the microwave but I feel that somehow it alters the taste ... makes it less creamy." He took a jar from a top shelf and showed it to Edward. "And, if you like, you can have hot chocolate."

"I don't know chocolate," admitted the boy.

"Then maybe it's time you tried it."

There was a light knock on the back door. Alex opened it to see his neighbour, Anne. She was quite attractive with long strawberry blonde hair and a few delicate freckles on her face. She oozed warmth and confidence even within that short space of time. Her nose wrinkled as she detected the aroma of the chocolate. "Mmm. I came into return this dish." She handed the article to Alex and easily maneuvered herself into the kitchen. Then she saw

Edward. "Oh, hello," she said to him. "Who might you be?"

"Edward," said Edward, simply.

"He's my nephew," Alex told her, sharing a glance with the boy.

"Ooh! How wonderful. And what a good looking boy too."

Edward remembered his semi naked chest and covered himself up.

"Oh don't worry about that sort of thing," Anne tittered, noticing his slight blush. "I'm very easy going, just ask your uncle. I'm Anne. I live next door."

"Would you like some hot chocolate, Anne?" Alex asked her.

"Love some," she said. "But another day. I have Eunice visiting and you know how she can be. Nice to meet you Edward. I'll see you later, Alex. Going off to Bath for a few days. Wanted to return the dish before I left. Don't let your milk run over."

Alex turned down the gas."

"Toodaloo, all," said Anne, slipping out the door again.

She was gone so quickly. Edward wrapped the cord around on his middle while Alex clicked the catch on the door. "She's always like that," he said. "But, hey, you've met a neighbour so you're official now. You live here."

"She must be nice because Arthur still didn't bark," said Edward,

"She is nice!" Alex turned off the gas and was about to pour hot milk into a mug when Edward suddenly clung onto him and hugged him tight. "Hey," Alex said gently. The boy was hiding his face in Alex's clothing, but Alex could feel the silent weeping. The effects of the day were spilling out. The little King had lost his battle with his emotions. All Alex could do was hold him until the storm inside the boy decided to settle down.

It was almost ten minutes before Edward could loosen his grip on Alex. Even then he held on to him, exhausted, slightly ashamed but thankful. Tears had dried but his heart felt like it was bursting. He knew he was no ghost.

This was no dream. He relaxed a little more. All this time Alex had held him in strong arms but said nothing. He felt himself floating. No he was being carried. He opened his eyes properly and saw the sofa drawing near. He allowed himself to drop onto it.

He had not considered the ceiling before. It was pale blue, not unlike a cloudless sky. A small chandelier with crystal drops hung above him. Alex was gone … but now he was back again with a mug of hot chocolate. Edward propped himself up on a cushion and accepted the drink with gratitude. Still no words. Alex sat on the char opposite him so that he was near but not intruding. The chocolate was dreamlike. If it had been a magic potion he could have died happy, but it was just a drink like nothing he had experienced before.

Eventually, Edward slept.

ക

Milly led them to a dingy looking building next to a walled garden. It had three full floors plus a clock tower which looked like it had been added as an afterthought. In some ways the building had the appearance of an old inn, including a sign which would have been swinging had there been any wind and if the sign had not been so worn and rusty. The ground floor windows had been blacked out. A chalk board at the entrance announced 'nude entertainment inside'.

"I can't go in because I'm only 16," said Milly. "But this is the place. He lives in the second floor. Just ask for Lucas."

"Why must you be over sixteen?" asked Robert.

"It's the rules," she told him, simply. "I'll wait in the café just a few doors that way." She pointed beyond the walled garden.

"I'll wait with you," said Megan. "This is not the best part of the city."

"This looks like a house of ill repute," said Ralph. "It is better that the ladies don't come in. How will we know this Lucas?"

"He has a mark on his forehead and wears a nose chain," Milly told him.

The knights entered the building which was dimly lit and quite smoke filled. There was a bar and tables not unlike a pub. A few people were inside and one gave the knights a suspicious glance. Robert returned the glance and the man averted his eyes and focused on his drink. The staircase was at the back. The barman studied the knights. "Are you looking for someone?" he asked.

"Lucas," said Robert.

"Oh, yeah, second floor at the back."

There was one yellowish lamp, looking like it was about to expire, on the first floor. The place smelled of furniture polish. The stairs were almost immediate. The knights took a few seconds to decide which way was the back. The room most likely had a bit of gum stuck in the keyhole. Robert knocked on the door and waited.

No answer, so Robert tried again, louder.

"Who is it?" came a voice.

"Are you Lucas?"

"Who wants to know?"

Robert frowned and opened the door. There was something wedged against the inside, so the knights forced their way in. Lucas was a thin man in his mid-twenties. His nose was running and he cowered liked a frightened animal.

"Leave me alone," he groaned. "I'll have the money tomorrow."

"We don't want your gold," Ralph told him. "Milly sent us."

"Milly?" Lucas gazed and sighed. "Milly, Milly. Sweet Milly." He looked up at the knights. "She ... she's kinda special, you know. I don't mean like, hot sexy special, although she's very very ... Do you like them young?"

"We are not here for cheap talk," said Robert. "She said you knew something that could help us in our quest."

"Quest? She said quest?"

"I say quest!"

Lucas smiled feebly "Then quest it is. Who am I to argue words?" He cleared his throat. "I must say you don't act like friends."

"We are not," said Robert. "But Milly is. Talk."

"Ok, but there's at least a pony in it? Yeah?"

"Just talk."

"Ok!" Lucas sat backwards on a chair. "I met this guy in the nick, about a year ago. We were shacked up together. Same cell. He's way older than I am but we got talking. In prison all you can do is talk. But he talked even in his sleep. Mostly rubbish, but he kept going on about stuff like kings and castles and treachery and stuff. I thought he was just a nut for history, but I told him about his night time rantings and he was totally, like, freaked. Anyway, I said not to worry. Prison messes with your head something serious."

Lucas paused as though he heard a sound on the floor. Once satisfied, he carried on. "He told me he was even older than he looked. Way older. He claimed to be about five hundred years ago. I mean … yeah, right. I just thought he was a bit cuckoo, but he said that if anything happened to him before he was released, to go to a certain place and find a certain thing. But he died a few months later."

"What certain thing?" asked Robert.

"I'm telling you, ok." Lucas listened to the sounds of the house and carried on. "Armour! A shield. A sword. A dagger. Real good ones, not like them cheap things you get in weird groups. And he said he used to serve someone called John Morton."

Ralph pondered on the name. "It could be the John Morton who we heard was sympathetic to our King. If he had people working to help restore Edward, this could have been one of them."

"Yes, Edward!" Lucas nodded. "Yes he used that name a few times in our chats."

"But he was old, you say." Robert was sceptical. "Would a man at arms, or a Knight, to be much older than us?"

"Aye, that's a good question?" agreed Ralph. "What happened to the armour?"

"Sold it," said Lucas. "A guy has to eat."

"So you have told us nothing," said Robert.

Lucas gazed at the knights. "Hey, hold on. Milly said you're looking for a kid called Edward who might be wearing stuff that looks like middle ages gear. This kinda fits, don't it?"

"The name Edward fits," said Ralph. "Nothing else."

"Swords and armour?" suggested Lucas.

"None of which you have," said Robert.

"Ah," Lucas wiped his nose on his cheek. "Well ... I do have one thing. Nobody wanted it but I kept it ... just in case. You never know how things might turn out." He crossed to a chest of drawers and fumbled around for a while, then found a small pouch. "It's got some kind of symbol but it's kinda rough."

Ralph took hold of it and showed it to Robert. "Tis the secret sign for the friends of Edward. It could only be known to a very few."

"So it's worth something to you?" Lucas asked hopefully.

"What was in the pouch?" asked Robert

"Nothing. If he ever had any money in it, he must have spent it."

"No messages?"

"Nope."

Ralph brought out a ten-pound note. He considered giving it to Lucas but then paused. "You are quite a sorry picture of a man. You need to improve. You bring dishonour to your family with each breath." He over handed the note.

"Two would be better," he muttered.

"Where was the armour buried?" asked Ralph. "Tell us the place and you shall have another."

"If you give me three I'll take you there," said Lucas. "But there is nothing there now. It has been built on, so you can't dig or anything but, yeah, I'll take you there for a look see … for the price."

"If there is nothing there, there is no point." Robert told him. "Just tell us how far and what the place in called."

"Well …"

"For one more of these notes," said Ralph.

"It's a place called Haggerston, near the railway."

"What was the name of the man who died?"

"He was called William Spence. At least that's the name he used."

Ralph handed over the note then turned the pouch inside out to examine it. There seem little more to be gained from this encounter. He tucked the pouch into his own pocket. William Spence was not a name the knights were familiar with, but if he had truly been a follow of John Morton it was unlikely the knights would have had much to do with him.

They left the room and could hear Lucas barricading the door again. A shadow moved on the staircase, quite briefly but very noticeable. It probably meant nothing. There were several people in the building, but the knights kept a careful watch as they descended the stairs. The lamp on the first floor was still making attempts to stay alive but all signs were that it was losing it's battle. There was a part of the floor which was almost in total darkness. The temptation to explore was strong, but the knights made their way back down to the ground floor.

A young woman was giving a nude performance. It was impossible for the knights to miss seeing her. It was not like they had never seen a nude dancer before, but it seemed like several lifetimes ago. Ralph watched her movements. She was light, supple, attractive in a crude sort of way and very alluring. The contours of her body, her smoothness, her delate navel called to him. It was easy to believe that such women were put on the earth to tempt the likes of him.

Robert thought she was too skinny. He gave Ralph a nudge and urged him outside. The evening sunlight dragged both of them into a different mood. Nobody seemed to be observing them, and nobody followed them to the café. The dingy building faded out of sight as they rounded the bend, and they were glad of it.

The café was preparing for closing but both knights had a coffee while they told Megan and Milly about the pouch. Ralph and Milly took sips from their cups at the same time. For some reason, tow even known to her, Milly felt a tingle when their eyes met. Ralph felt only surprise that such a slight glance could light any fire within him. Maybe he was seeing Milly but remembering the nude dancer. He took another sip. He wanted to say something totally unremarkable, but he felt too blank.

She was smiling to herself without noticing. She saw Megan looking at her, then realised Megan was saying something. Was she blushing? She was hoping not. It was just a casual fantasy within a careless thought. It did not mean anything. "What?" she asked Megan.

"What made you hook up with a toe-rag like Lucas anyway?"

"Dunno," shrugged Milly. "It just happened, I guess."

"Hmm," Megan checked to see if there were any dregs left in her cup. "You can do much better."

Milly had an involuntary glance at Ralph, and then at Robert. "I know," she said. "He's just a kinda friend that's all."

"Some friend!"

The café was now definitely closing. The group filtered out and made plans for tomorrow. The knights were used to long hours but, somehow, time travel had begun to wear on them. Ralph spoke quietly to Robert. "Since this afternoon I have been feeling a weight of emotion building up. Worse this evening with the nude woman and then, for a moment, with Milly. Have you felt anything similar?"

"Indeed," said Robert. "But not, perhaps, as strongly as you have. Maybe, if we have truly travelled the road of time, it is a normal effect."

"It is quite unsettled," admitted Ralph. "I can only hope that it does not put our quest in jeopardy."

"We must stand strong and assist each other."

"Yes," Despite himself, Ralph yawned. "Maybe a break until morning would be the best thing for now. Tomorrow is always another day."

Morning After

The chandelier was still there, coming softly into focus above him. He gazed at it for a while as his thoughts began to wake up. The now familiar hum of the city faded in from his slumber. If he had dreamed during the night, he could not remember any of it. He was still on the sofa, still in his karate style dressing gown. There was music coming from somewhere nearby, and he could hear his brother humming along with an occasional word from Alex. So, yesterday had really happened.

A wet, rough tongue brushed his face. Edward sat up. Stroked Arthur and stretched. There were still signs on the opposite chair that Alex had spent the night there, watching over the boy. A mirror on one wall reflected Edward. He tidied his hair and fastened the cord on his dressing gown, then followed the sounds from the kitchen.

Richard was tucking into beans on toast like many other kids that morning. The brothers shared a silent greeting. The clock on the wall said it was seven thirty Six. Edward listened to the music and tried to work out where it was coming from. Richard tapped the radio / CD player. "It's not magic," he grinned.

"Sit down, Edward," Alex invited him. "Would you like some beans for breakfast?"

"They are good," assured Richard.

So, the little King began his first normal morning in the twenty first century. It was not quite like being reborn, but Edward thought that was possibly close to how he felt. A song on the radio was celebrating Summer. A slight breeze was now coming through the window. Richard was happy. Maybe he had purposely pushed the negativities of the last few days from his mind. Nobody could blame him for that. It was good to see him smiling again; to hear him laughing again.

After breakfast, Edward tested the shower. He spent quite a while under it, using the gel and loofa, then wiping the steam from the mirror and looking at himself. Then he lingered over selecting his wardrobe for the day, trying different styles. He could not work out what to do with the ties, even though Miles had thoughtfully put some pictures on the inside of the doors. Eventually, Edward chose to be casual with cream trousers and a deep blue short sleeved shirt.

The list of Kings on his wall did make him feel a bit unreal. The picture they had used for him was not accurate, but nor was the one of his father. It didn't matter much. The next Edward was also young. He wondered if the very name of Edward was a bad omen for a King. None of them seemed to have been King for very long. He put the thoughts of Kingship aside and went into the library.

Richard was there, cross legged on the floor, flipping through a picture book. He was not as an avid reader as his brother was. He could manage words well enough but, today, he was too relaxed to be bothered. The book showed great inventions over the centuries. He was learning a lot of basic stuff which he suspected most kids half his age would know already. He had a good excuse, but he knew he had to try and catch up without his brain frying.

Edward sat in an armchair and looked up at the various shelves. He remembered the 'Ghost of Greyminster' book which had seen yesterday. He found it and was soon engrossed. He hardly noticed when Arthur wandered in and rested his head on the boy's knee.

It was Thursday. Alex was happy to give the brothers some space. They could all visit Miles in the afternoon but, now, it was a time relax and adjust. A shape cast a shadow beside the front door. It stayed for a moment but then moved away. Alex had a casual look through the window but saw only the back of a man's head. Then Arthur barked. Just a short bark followed by a low grumble. Someone was not welcome.

Richard looked out of the library window and saw the back of the man walking away. This was still a strange place, but it was comfortable and, he thought, safe. He tried to put aside all his previous fears. All that had happened to jerk the morning was that Arthur had barked. Dog's do that. He settled himself down on the floor again.

"What was that?" asked Edward, looking up.

"Nothing much," Richard told him.

❧

The view from their window really wasn't very pretty, thought Ralph, as he munched on a bagel. Robert had brought some from the small café next door, along with coffee in two strange white cup which refused to burn their hands but kept the liquid hot. Again, the coffee tasted slightly different but none, so far, had been undrinkable.

Ralph studied the pouch again, now that he was feeling more refreshed. "If this William had come from near our time, and was truly working for the good of Edward," he pondered. "What does that mean for our situation. I mean … he was older so, does that mean he was already older when he arrived in our time, or did he come from a few years different to us?" He considered his words. "That sounded odd!"

Robert did not like the idea of time travel at all. Wizardry! It's all evil. He had always said as much. "Maybe this Lucas knows more than he was saying. We both let him off lightly. I say we pay him another visit."

"I think we paid him too much already," said Ralph.

Robert half smiled. "Maybe you are too afraid to see that temptress again. I agree she had a good body."

"Oh, you noticed that, did you?"

The both laughed.

"And I think Milly has eyes for you," observed Robert.

"I think she has eyes for us both," said Ralph.

"She is a mere child," said Robert. "But pleasing to look at. Give her another few years and she could make a fine wife."

"But by then you'll be too old," smiled Ralph.

"I'll never get old," said Robert. "Apparently, I'm already over five hundred, and I still feel young."

A car back fired, causing the knights to rush to the window. They had both seen gunpowder tested in The Tower when they had served the old King. This sound was similar and they were surprised when they saw the car was undamaged. No explosion, just smoke. Ralph returned his attention to the pouch. "Suppose this William was intercepted on a message. The same wizard who sent us and our King, and young Richard, into this other time could have sent him too. But why do that instead of just killing us?"

"He did not kill us because we gave him no chance," said Robert.

"Aye, but he did not kill Edward or Richard so." Ralph sat on a chair and wondered about that. "Maybe he cannot kill. Maybe there is something which denies him the power to kill."

"That would be an amazing advantage for us," said Robert. "To have an opponent who cannot kill."

"Or …" An idea flashed in Ralph's mind but it was nearly gone in an instant. He cleared his head and tried to get it back. It was almost as if some force was preventing him from focusing. "I had it then. God help me. It made sense for moment but …"

"I hate when that happens," said Robert.

It was gone! Ralph knew it might be back, if he stopped trying to think about it. He hoped it would. He looked back out the window where people were gathering near the gates of the school. The building did not appear so grim as it had yesterday. The graffiti was more like art now, a mural with pictures of flowers and birds. Some many things looked different now. He saw Milly crossing the road, then stopping at the kerb, somehow sensing his presence and smiling up at him. She had not forgotten their connection. He had not meant to smile back, but it happened anyway.

The emotions were not so strong as before, but he still felt a thrill at her arrival. She came up, lightly skipping like a small child. He hoped she had news for them, partly because that would detract from the thrill, but mostly because he had not lost track from their main purpose. He hoped she had not also.

"I'm meeting Amber in about an hour," she said, keeping her eyes on Ralph. "We chatted on Twitter. She said she gave Edward her number."

"Number?" asked Robert.

She glanced at him then. "Phone number. You ... either of you ... don't know about phones, do you?"

"We just haven't used them before," admitted Ralph.

"Wow!" She met his gaze and held it, then looked away. "You really are from somewhere else!" She looked at them in turn, then focused on Ralph. "But I know you're good. That's the main thing."

Robert noted her interest in Ralph and smiled faintly. "Tell us more about Lucas." He said. "What does he do for a living."

She sat on the sofa. "He doesn't actually have a job as such. He's a bit of a hustler. Always has been. He shared a flat with by brother for about a year. Then he ..." She lowered her voice, the way people do when sharing something as though it's a secret but the whole world knows about it already. "He was in prison. Not for nothing real bad, just kinda pushing and stuff. He can be nice when you get to know him."

"Does he ever hurt you?" asked Ralph. He had to know that.

"No." She looked deep into his eyes. "No, never. Nothing like that."

"Good." Ralph could feel her breath. He forced himself to move farther away from her. "We'll come with you to where you meet Amber. We won't get involved unless you need us too. We'll just be nearby."

"Okay." She seemed to say it feebly. Had she noticed that he'd moved away from her. He offered her a smile and she blushed. "Can I use your whatsit?"

They both looked at her questioningly. Robert took a shot at it. "Yes," he said.

She went through the door and they understood. Robert let out a laugh. "Your face is a picture. You have got it bad!"

"It wasn't planned," assured Ralph. "Maybe it's the time thing still affecting me."

"Or maybe it's simply that you have fallen for her."

"In a day?"

"It's been known to happen."

"Not to me." His face grew solemn. "Maybe someone slipped me a love potion."

Robert chuckled. "It's quite funny but, as I said earlier, she's of age and quite pretty. So there are worse things that could happen."

Ralph sighed and rubbed his face. "For now we have to put all else aside until we find out King. This number. Maybe we should ask about getting one."

"Not me," said Robert. "I think those numbers are to do with the way people seem to talk to themselves. I do not want to get caught up with that."

"Then I'll just get one," said Ralph. "If they help to find the King then I am all for them. You are too suspicious."

Milly returned. She knew that they had been talking about her, but she was not worried about that. It was good that they liked her. She hoped Ralph liked her the most. She was certain he did. "If Megan is late coming, I'll go there alone and you can find me. I'm meeting Amber, and I think Michelle, in Weaver's Fields. That place we were at yesterday."

"We know the place," said Robert. "If Megan is late, you can walk there with Ralph. It's good to have an escort in times like these."

Her smile widened. Ralph saw the sense in plan and prepared himself to stay focused. If Megan is much later, meaning Robert would be too and, if anything did happen ... though it was unlikely anything would ... he would have to deal things single handed. But ... maybe Amber will bring the King with her. That would really win the day.

"I like the idea of a man watching over me," said Milly. "But I came here in my own, remember. It's not like I need a guy to with me all the time."

"Indeed," agreed Robert. "It's merely an offer."

But Megan did arrive, as they all believed she would. She had left the old man sleeping. He could sleep hours or just minutes, so she made sure he had someone, from their squat, with him. If he got confused and tried to walk to their old building he could end up in Ilford.

"We are all here," said Megan. "That's good."

✥

Alex could have forgotten that there were young boys in the house. They were so quiet. He reminded himself that there were Royal children, but boys are boys. He knew because he used to be one. Even Royal brothers must argue sometimes. Maybe, once they were settled in, they would start behaving as normal. Edward seemed to accepted that he was not King in this England of 2016, but that would, surely, need some time for adjustment.

Now Alex saw Edward in the doorway, like a reflection of last evening. The boy was watching him, one hand on the dog's fur. After a minute, Edward sat on the sofa and sorted his hair before speaking.

"Thank you for being so understanding, last night," said Edward.

"That's okay. We all have moments when we need understanding."

Edward dusted his shirt and glanced at himself in the mirror. "What does okay mean?" He asked.

"It just means all right."

"I heard a few people say it." Edward picked a fluff off his trousers. "Alex ... you know that number?"

"Amber's number?"

"Yes." Edward was not sure why he blushed.

"You want to call her?"

The boy hesitated but then said "Yes, but ... I'm a bit nervous. Not of Amber, but ... I've got no idea how to use that thing."

"The thing is called a phone," said Alex. "It's nothing to worry about. My father still doesn't like to use it, but he can if he needs to."

"Oh." Edward had run out of things to adjust so he settled for stroking Arthur. "I would like to call her. Yes."

Alex picked up the house phone and pressed a few numbers. He handed it to Edward. "Just listen to that for now. Get used to the feel."

The boy listened to a recorded message. "It sounds funny."

Alex laughed. "It's me. My house phone in York. Once you hear something like a high whistle, say hello."

Edward held the phone close to his ear and shouted. "HELLO."

"You don't need to shout through it, just talk normal. Say it again."

"Hello."

Alex took the phone from him and switched it off. "That's all there is to it.

"oh," He smiled and then said. "Okay."

Alex patted the boy's shoulder then handed the phone back to him. "To call Amber just press the numbers in the right order then press the red button. Then wait until she answers."

Edward memorised the instructions. It seemed easy enough. He disappeared upstairs, then came back with his address book and a smile. He wanted to use the phone while Alex was with him until he felt confidant. He pressed the buttons and waited, not quite understanding why his mouth was suddenly dry.

"*Hello?*" It was Amber!

He forgot his name and looked to Alex for help.

"Edward!" Alex reminded him.

"I'm Edward. Hello."

"*Oh Wow. Hey. Sup?*"

What? "Erm ... how are you?"

"*I'm meeting some girl called Milly in a bit.*"

"What? Oh okay."

"*She was asking about you. About the pic on Facebook.*"

"Oh ... I don't know a girl called Milly."

"*Where are you? At home?*"

"Yes." The word just came to him and it stopped him for a few seconds. Home! "Yes. I'm at home." It made him smile but also made him feel sad.

"*You want to meet some time?*"

"Yes. When? Today maybe?" He felt a tingle inside.

"*Yeah, sure. We're going to the park now. Could meet you there if you want.*"

Edward guessed the 'we' meant Michelle and Shelley, or maybe Milly. He looked at Alex and put dropped the phone a few inches. "Could I meet Amber at the park?"

"You'd get lost very easy from here," Alex told him. "Ask her where she is and say you live in Stepney."

Edward held up the phone again. "Amber? I'm in Stepney. Where are you?"

"*You live in Stepney? Oh Wow! That is so amazing. I live in Stepney too. Do you know White Horse Lane?*"

"Erm ... Is that anywhere near the retail park?" Edward felt quite proud of himself for remembering that landmark.

"*You kidding? I live like just a short walk from that. You live near that?*"

"Just yards from it," said Edward, loving the enthusiasm in her voice.

"*We so have to meet. I'll call you later, yeah. Today. That okay?*"

"Yes. I'd like that."

"Cool. See you later then. Luv yah."

"Okay. Yes." Edward heard a buzz and he knew her call was over. He knew he was smiling. He sighed and rested back on the sofa. He had never felt this kind of thrill before. He handed the phone back to Alex.

"I guess you like her," said Alex, watching Edward's face.

"Yes." The boy blushed. "Does 'luv yah' mean the same as 'I love you'?"

"Not quite. It's a sign of affection, but not the same as total love."

"Oh."

"But, if she said it to you it means she likes you, in some way."

"I understand, I think."

"You have just met her once."

"I kissed her!"

"I saw."

"You were watching us?"

"I saw you," said Alex. "That's one of the things that made me wonder if you really were the boys I was waiting for. All I had to go on was your clothing."

"Yes, I suppose." Edward stroked Arthur's hair softly. "I think my father would have approved, if … if things were different."

Richard came into the room and joined his brother on the sofa. "When do we see Miles again?" he asked.

"This afternoon." Alex sorted some papers and magazines beside his chair. "Hopefully, he will be able to come home soon. I'll ask the doctors today."

"I hope so," said Richard.

"Me too," said Edward.

Arthur, who had been relaxing at Edward's feet tensed and rumbled. He wandered towards the front door and sat looking and listening. There was nobody outside that could be seen, but there was something which disturbed the air. All of his senses were focusing on the something, but he did not know what it was.

Alex looked out the window, then opened the door. Apart from a neighbour washing his car, the road was clear. Arthur sniffed the ground and glanced across at the tree lined garden opposite. He gave a few more rumbles. Alex gave the dog a pat. "There's nothing there," he commented. "Maybe thunder somewhere."

Edward joined them at the door. He immediately was aware of eyes focusing on him from somewhere up above. He scanned the upstairs windows and rooftops, then spied the culprit. A boy, barely visible in the branches, no older than ten years. Edward crossed the road and went into the garden to get a closer.

"Were you watching us?" he asked the boy.

"No law against it." The boy stayed in the trees.

"What's your name?"

"What's yours?"

"I'm Edward."

The boy looked him over again. "I'm John. Where do you live?"

Edward pointed to the house. "You saw where I was living."

"You didn't use to live there. I not seen you before."

"I just moved in ... with my uncle." Edward was getting tired of looking up at him. "Come down."

"You come up," Challenged the John. "If you can climb."

It was an old ash tree. Edward took grip and hoisted himself up and in, then settled himself on the branch. His cream trousers got a bit scuffed but, although he been born to be King, he was a boy first. He took a better look at John. "Where do you live?"

John hesitate for a second then pointed towards the junction. "A couple of streets away. "You got any brothers or sisters?"

"Yes," said Edward, deciding to be coy.

"Bet you got a brother," said John. "Saw him through the window earlier."

"So you been watching us for a while?"

"I watch everybody," said John, almost proudly.

"You upset our dog!"

"Naw." John shrugged off the accusation. "That weren't me. I been sitting here loads of times and your dog hasn't made a fuss."

A squirrel moved in the next tree. It stopped and considered the boys for a moment, then went about it's normal business. "Bet I know what it was though," said John with a smile. He pointed to a house on the other side of the walled garden. "See that low kinda shed thingy. The guy who owns that house uses that shed for making stuff. He's a kinda inventor. All kinds of weird sounds come from there and I bet he's made something that only dogs can hear. Like them whistle things."

Edward considered that John might just be pulling his leg, but he now knew that strange things, wizards, inventions and such, did exist. He had mixed feelings about the possibility of a wizard living so close to his home. It was unlikely that is would be the same wizard but … he noticed that John was stifling a laugh. "You're making that up!"

"Yep." The laugh escaped. "Your face. You really believe that rubbish."

Edward felt himself flush. "It's not funny."

"It is kinda."

Briefly, Edward hated him. Then he didn't mind him. Then he relaxed and quite liked him. It was good to connect with a local kid. It made the world feel just a bit less alien. He suspected that, if he had met John in his old year of 1483 he would have dismissed him as just a peasant. Or maybe John would have been a spy, like the one they had found and viciously flogged outside of the castle walls last year. Edward shuddered at the memory. He had given ordered that nobody so young should ever be flogged to such an extent again, no matter what the crime.

John began to climb down from the tree. "I got to go now. Might see you soon." He added as an afterthought. "But it will be before you see me." He dropped down and waited until Edward had done the same, then he gave a cheeky smile and set off towards the gate.

Encounters

Weavers Fields was like a battle zone in reverse, strewn with live people, carefree, sunning themselves, reading, talking, playing while the Summer sun beat down upon them. Where Robert and Ralph had first arrived, a junior football game was now in progress. Ice cream cones and iced lollies were in heavy demand. Two teenage girls were practicing violin beside one of the benches. There was even a boy trying to fly a kite despite the lack of sufficient wind.

Megan had bought, using Ralph's money, pairs of sunglasses for each of the knights. Robert kept his is tucked in his jacket pocket but Ralph tried his on and was still wearing them as they entered the park. They were strange but he liked them. Milly sent a text to Amber to wait by the central café. It was not a superhot day but it was warm enough the men shed their shirts and make women wish they could. The knights had intention of following suit.

Weather did not seem to effect Megan. She had her own form of cool. There were a few wisps of cloud in the sky. Megan studied those for a minute until she saw a middle aged man going from person to person, begging change. Eventually, he reached Megan. She nudged him. "Get lost, Denny," she told him. "It's me, you dork."

He blinked at her. "Oh! Hi Megan. Didn't know you were working this patch."

"I'm not." She shook her head at him. "And you're not pot less either. You got your benefit yesterday."

"Well," He shrugged. "Them that have can afford to give more to them what haven't. That's what I say."

Megan beckoned him closer. "You haven't seen a couple of boys wearing gear like they were frim the middle ages, have you?"

"When?"

"Yesterday."

"Naw, I was down the club yesterday. Why, what they done."

"They've done nothing," she told him. "We were just looking for them, that's all."

"Naw ... I see them other guys though. The ones the rozzers are after." He lowered his voice. "Heard they duffed up two of them. I saw them hopping off that way. Weird so-and-sos they were."

Megan smirked at the knights. "Yes, real weird. But not all bad I bet."

"You think not?" Denny shrugged again. "Well ... I guess maybe not. I never told the rozzers I saw them though, so it'd matter much."

Megan gave him a pat. "You take care, okay."

"You too Meg." Denny returned to his begging.

Milly's phone beeped. She listened for a while, her face straightening with each new breath. If it was news relating to Amber, it could not be good, but it was something else. She sucked in her breath and then let it out again slowly. "I know ... Yes, but ... they'll never do that ... but you've got to, now." She glanced at the knights. "I can't promise you nothing, okay ... I'll try ... Lucas? ... damn!" She sighed and hugged her phone, then turned to the knights. "Can you guys do something for me?"

"Do what?" asked Robert.

"You remember Lucas from last night?"

Robert frowned. "An unworthy friend."

"Yes," she agreed. "But a friend just the same. He's in trouble."

"What kind of trouble?" asked Ralph.

"He owes money. He got in with the wrong crowd … again." She looked at them for some level of understanding. "He says they are going to kill him, okay."

Robert felt little sympathy. "Cannot he go to what you call rozzers?"

"It may be his better choice of action," said Ralph.

"Maybe." Milly was not hopeful. "He's never been very lucky with them." She looked up at Ralph. "Please. For me? Can't you go help him."

"It is not our quest," said Ralph. "He has other options. It might not be right for us to help him when he refuses to help himself."

"Indeed," agreed Robert.

"So you won't help?" Milly stared at them, but mostly at Ralph. "I'm helping you with your quest, so why not help me with mine?"

"It would not be yours," said Robert.

"But," Ralph swapped glances with Robert. "Yours is a fair point. Forgive us, sweet lady. Where will we find Lucas?"

Milly looked into his eyes then kissed him lightly. "Lucas might not thank you but I do. Both of you. He'll be in the same place as last night, unless they have driven him out, somehow."

"Who will we be up against?" asked Robert.

Her phone beeped. "I don't know really. Wait." She saw that she had a text from Amber. "Amber is coming into the park now. I'll do the best for you, if you do your best for me."

The knights instinctively looked around in case they could see Edward and Richard with any of the girls entering the park. Megan gave Milly a soft hug. "I'll wait here for you, okay." She watched Milly cross the park towards a children's play area, then she turned to the knights. "Whoever the people may be, they could be tough. There are some not very nice people in the city, so be careful."

"We are used to dealing with people who are not very nice," Robert told her, with a half smile. "It's what I, for one, was born for."

"I can believe it," said Megan. "Oh ... just don't kill anyone, okay. You can't do that in this century."

"As a knight, I try not to do that in any century," he said. "But there are always those who oppose justice and peace. However, shall try to heed your words."

⁕

The garden at the back of Alex's house was in full bloom and the birds were singing. It was smaller than the garden at The Tower but had a pleasing atmosphere. Edward decided to stay within call of Alex for the moment. Most of his life had been supervised and monitored for one reason or other. He had survived his time around Weavers Fields, short as it was, but it had made him realised how restricted, and how protected, his life had been. Now he had more freedom to roam but he was not too confidant of roaming far. His experienced with Tiger had been a bit of an eye opener. His first combat. He just thought he should take things slowly.

He had found a book on England, with photos of notable castles and great houses, which he was now reading. His home, Ludlow Castle, was now a ruin. It had made him sad for a while. Some many people had gone, lost in history, but there was nothing he could do about that. He was done crying for things that could never be changed. He could love this garden. He could learn to love this new England.

The current Queen had a pleasant smile. He understood why she could never know about him. He had a new life. Miles had drawn up a plan, papers and documents which had been sitting in a desk for all these years, waiting for his approval. Edward York was a fitting name. He was part of the House of York. In essence, he was the last King of the House of York. He reflected on that while watching a ladybird settle on a leaf.

Richard brought him a glass of lemonade and they both sat on the grass to enjoy their drinks. Something shifted in the sunlight. They each sheltered their eyes against the glare to see who was moving.

"Hello there," came a happy voice. "How are you today?"

It was Anne. Edward sat up so he could see her better. "Hello," he replied. "I thought you were going to Bath."

"Not until tonight, dear. The best laid plans, and all that, what." She leaned on the fence. "Who's this then?"

"My brother, Richard."

"Oh, how wonderful. Pleased to meet you, Richard. Or do you prefer Rick?"

The younger brother looked her over. "Richard!" he said.

"Where do you live when not in London?" she asked them.

Edward joined her at the fence. "I was living in Wales," he said, truthfully.

"Oh, nice. Lots of hills and sheep." She winked at him. "Yes, I do detect a faint accent. So, you're staying here for summer? Taking in the sights and things?"

"I suppose so," said Edward, not wanting to say anything out of turn.

"Come here, dear." Anne called Richard over to him. "Let me have a good look at you. Oh, my … you are absolutely adorable. Both of you. Such a shame I'm going away for a few days. How long are you staying here? I hope I get to see you again."

Richard let her kiss him, though it was a bit wet. "We are staying here a while," he said.

Anne saw the book on the ground. "I see you have a book on castles. Are you interested in history, or just castles?"

"Both, I suppose," Edward told her.

"You've probable been to The Tower already," she said, casually.

The brothers looked at each other and just nodded. Edward took a sip of his drink. "I prefer Ludlow Castle," he told her. "I have better memories of that."

An air ambulance come in sight above them. The boys watched it, lightly mesmerized, as it glided across the skyline until it was swallowed up by the city. Edward took a long drink from his glass. People travelled by flying things, he had learned that through the past amazing twenty four hours, but he still didn't understand how it worked. Richard's imagination was in full flow. To fly like a bird would be an amazing adventure.

"Have you ever flown?" he asked Anne.

She smiled at his obvious enthusiasm on the subject. "Oh, yes, lots of times."

"Really? What's it like?"

"I've only done Europe, so just short trips. Not like going to Australia or even America. It's just like being in a bus."

Richard wanted to ask where those places were, but Anne's tone suggested they were too well known for him to not know about, so he stopped himself. He could not hear the helicopter now. "I would like to ride on one of those," he said.

"Maybe you will," she told him. "One day."

⚜

The knights leaned against a short wall just across the road from the place where they had been told they would find Lucas. The building was still dingy and appeared to be locked. The sign about nude entertainment was gone. The situation was unusual. It was against their better judgment to get involved at all, but they had given their word of honour to Milly.

"So, we just watch and wait, to see what he is up to," said Ralph. "I don't believe he asked for us because he likes us. There is something peculiar about his intentions."

They were aware that he would be able to see them from where they were waiting. Time would tell if Lucas had the patience or intelligence to match their own. Maybe the sight of them without action would dismay him enough. But, what was going through his mind?

"If it is as you suspect," said Robert. "He must have others who is in contact with. Do you think Milly is in league?"

Ralph shook his head. "No, she is innocent. Too innocent, perhaps. She tries to see only the good in him."

"Are you sure you are not just sweet on her?"

"I considered that." Ralph looked at him. "She has the same glint in her eyes as my Mary had, and a similar tone of voice. I realise that now. But … yes I like her. She is a fine lady and will be party to any wrong doing. He is using her."

"If she does manage to point us to our King, she will have performed a good service," said Robert. "So I hope you are right."

They watched as the latest of a string of buses stopped to let people get on and off. This was an experience the knights had not known yet, but the prospect did not fill them with enthusiasm. They preferred their horses, with the wind in their hair and the sun on their backs. A couple of young boys on skateboards kept them entertained for a few minutes.

"I can imagine Adam trying to master that skill, if he was here," said Ralph. "I wonder what he is doing now. He should have worked out that we were not coming back, so should be on his way to his father's estate by now."

"I wonder what England is like back there," said Robert. "Do they know that Edward is missing? From what we have been told, nobody knows what happened to him, but I suspect a number of people do know, or at least suspect."

"They suspect he was murdered," confirmed Ralph. "Nobody would really suspect anything so strange as this." He nudged Robert and pointed out that the main door of the building had been opened. Lucas and two other men came out. They glanced quickly in the direction of the knights and then set off along the road away from them.

"This is it," said Ralph.

They followed slowly, boldly, crossing the road between the cars, past a row of shops. Once or twice, Lucas looked back to check if the knights were still following. They all halted at a side road where one of the men seemed to be using a mobile phone. Then they turned up the side road. Several buildings were boarded up, and others were in construction. Artwork attempted to relieve the monotony of the area. A large sketch of a boy picking his nose was one of the highlights of the block.

"I think, if anything of significance is going to happen," said Ralph. "It will be in the next few moments." He felt to make sure he still had his small dagger.

Most of the buildings that were finished were offices. They soon arrived at a cul de sac. Lucas and the two men stopped to face the knights. One of the men, slightly taller than the other, wearing a grey casual suit, stepped forward. "Greeting, gentlemen," he smiled. "It seems you have an interest in us."

"And you, in us," said Ralph.

Two more men stepped into the road behind the knights.

"I'm called Lance," said the grey suit. "Interesting name, considering your history. I am right that you have used lances ... in the past."

The knights shared a glance. Ralph nodded to himself. "So, our secret is out. Was it the pouch, the sign of Edward?"

"In part." Lance had an easy manner which most likely masked a much darker side. "We knew you had come. The job you did on the police officers! It was obvious you did not understand where you had arrived, at first, and ... our boss ... lost track of you. Time travel is a confusing thing. Although you stepped through into that wonderful purple mist last, you actually arrived first. Lucas, among others, was asked to put out feelers. Intelligence, as you know, is a vital part of any campaign."

"So what is your plan now?" asked Robert.

Lance smiled softly. "Simply to stop you from preventing our plan." He brought out a pistol. "This weapon is perhaps strange to you. It fires a small object into the body, and can cause death. We don't have to use one on you two. If things go as we hope ..." He stopped and put the pistol back into his pocket. "I must not give too much away. I am from this generation and, possibly, have seen too much TV. I know the 'bad guys' don't always get away with it. That's what you would think we are. 'Bad guys'. But ..."

"Where is our King?" asked Robert abruptly.

Lance smiled again. "He is safe. We know where he is and, when the time is right, we shall make use of him. But we have no intention to harm him."

"What then?" asked Ralph.

"You simply do not need to know." Lance directed most of his conversion to Ralph, choosing him as his main opponent. "I know it's all about honour for people like you, but things have changed over the centuries. Honour plays little part in today's England." He looked closely as Ralph. "You are just a normal man without armour and no shield. Just forget Edward. You owe him nothing. Walk away. Make a life for yourselves. I know there were others from your time who came here. At least one is dead. The others may be also. You have no third man to watch your backs. Your quest was doomed before it began."

"How do I know Edward is safe?" asked Ralph. "If I can be certain ..."

"Oh, yes. He is safe. He made some friends already. You know that, or you heard it." Lance looked Ralph straight in the eye. "You can rest easy."

Ralph returned his gaze. "I don't think so."

Lance lost his smile. "Then you're a fool!"

A tittering from nearby. They all followed the sound to the old man seated on a wall. "Foolish is as foolish does," he chanted.

Lance laughed. "Oh, you do have a third man. Well done."

The old man tittered again. "Three in a row times three is nine."

One by one, six more men emerged from the side road. They were a raggedly bunch, not well washed, but all able bodied and much younger than the old man. A young boy with a mop of red hair and one front tooth missing, hopped onto the wall beside the old man.

Lance looked briefly surprised and pulled out his pistol again. "You lot can all back off," he said. "This has nothing to do with you." He saw Robert move, but too late to stop the fist that plunged into his face. Lance was laid out cold, the pistol sent swinging from his hand. Ralph grabbed it; not because he wanted to use it, but he did not want anyone else to use it.

A pellet from the young boy's slingshot hit Lucas and the other three men were attacked the raggedly bunch. Fists and feet were engaged in a fierce battle for a few minutes. Robert grabbed hold of Lucas and pinned him in place. The old man stayed on the wall, jerking and enjoying every blow he was witnessing. The boy had a good aim and struck home several times before Ralph signalled that they should let the three victims go. They had Lance and Lucas. That was enough to force the truth.

The boy dropped down beside Ralph. "The rozzers will be coming soon. You best dump that somewhere." He pointed to the pistol. "Wipe it and lobbed it up on a roof." When Ralph hesitated, the boy fished through Lance's pockets and found a hanky. He took the pistol, wiped it with the hanky and then threw it high so that disappeared into the construction site. "There!" he said. "Now they can't nab you for it."

"Thank you," said Ralph.

"You should have emptied it first," said a large member of the raggedly bunch.

"You find it and you do that then," said the boy.

Robert still had hold of Lucas. "If the rozzers are coming then we should move. Where is the best place nearby?"

"Take them to the old carwash," said the large raggedly man. "I'll carry this one," He picked up Lance as if he was a feather, and he led the way over a wire fence to a disused building.

"I didn't plan anything of this," assured Lucas. "They made me do it. I'm really with you guys."

Robert pushed Lucas into a corner and sat over him. "You knew about it. You lured us into it. You are very much a part of it," Robert told him. "You are totally without honour."

"Stop going on about honour," said Lucas. "This is the real world. Everybody is in it for whatever they can get. Why should I be any different? I need to eat and have some fun. That doesn't make me evil."

Ralph also stood over him. "Milly is a fair maiden. She saw you as a friend, but you are no friend. You just use her."

"I always treated her proper," insisted Lucas. "And I never laid a finger on her."

"So, do the right thing now," urged Ralph. "Tell us all about Lance and what plans he had."

"He never told me anything important. He mostly treated me like scum. He never trusted me."

"But you were with him, and you helped try to lure us into his trap."

Lucas looked away. "That was for money. He didn't say anything about that Edward, or plans for power, or anything that would help your quest."

Robert pulled Lucas closer and looked him in the eye. "Why did you say power?"

"I didn't."

Robert punched him. "Speak the truth."

"Okay! You …" Lucas wondered if he could taste blood. "All I know is that he's working for a guy who want's some kind of power. Like I said, he don't trust me enough."

Ralph remembered the pouch and approached the old man. He showed him the pouch. "Do you recognise this?"

Old eyes scanned the item and a flicker of light dawned within. "Tis the sign of Edward," he muttered.

Ralph and Robert exchanged glances. "So, you have seen it before?"

"What? Seen what before?"

"This pouch."

The old man looked at it as though for the first time. "Is there food in it?"

Ralph sighed and tried again. "You said the sign of Edward."

"Yes," agreed the old man. "That's his sign. That's what it means."

"Do you remember a William Spence?" asked Ralph.

"No," replied the old man. "But there lots I don't remember."

Ralph took back the pouch and patted the old man on the shoulder. "Try to think about it, but don't let it bother you."

Lance started to recover. He sat up and looked around, wondering where he was, then he saw Robert. He felt his chin and tested his jaw. The old building was one he did not recognise but, as he grew more aware, he knew the sounds of the city. "You didn't have to hit me," he said.

"Oh, but I did," Robert told him. "And I shall gladly hit you again should the need arise. Tell us where we shall find our King. Also tell us who you are working for."

Lance shot an angry glance at Lucas. "It would be a waste of time. He cannot be touched by the likes of you. You have no idea! He is so far above you."

"About his plans, then," urged Ralph.

"Go suck a hedgehog."

Robert knocked him out again.

Kings and Stuff

Edward had Alex's mobile phone with him. He was studying in; playing with it, getting the feel of it. He was just on the corner of his street, opposite the retail park. Arthur was with him. Several people had passed by him and he was getting used to being an almost invisible member of the public. There was nothing particular to make him stand out from the crowd, but he still felt a little awkward.

He had elected to go on his own to meet Amber. She had phoned, and they had arranged to meet in just a few minutes. He was nervous. Butterflies were dancing inside his chest to the rhythm of his heartbeat. He hoped she would still be as gorgeous and exquisite as he remembered. It had only been on day but his emotions had been tried to their limits so he did not fully trust them.

The traffic no longer alarmed him. Cars buzzed by him without a twinge. He kissed Arthur and patted his coat as he waited. He was still not sure what the retail park was for but it seemed to be a center of operations for some kind. Cars came and went. He watched the activities quite passively for some time.

Then there she was, like a princess. She was still wearing shorts and crop top. He tried not to look at her navel but felt drawn to her body. It was like a battle inside of him, against all that he learned from his priests and advisors. She was smiling. Waving to him as she approached. Then they were together. He remembered the kiss. It was not like the kiss between the couple he had witnessed in Weavers Fields, but ...

"Hi!" she said. She ruffled Arthur's fur and then her eyes met Edward's. She linked arms with him. "I still can't believe that you live so close to me."

He was transfixed by her beauty. He wanted to freeze this moment forever, but then he noticed the way she was looking at him. He smiled as casually he could. "Yes. I did not know either." He led the way to the house and liked the way she gasped when she saw it.

"This is where you live?"

"Yes, but it's not mine until I'm eighteen."

"What?" She gazed at him. "You will own it when you're eighteen? That is ... amazing."

He felt proud, but he did not know why. He opened the front door for her and loved the way she whistled. He liked everything about her. He composed himself suddenly. He was host. He had been King. He should not act like an awed pup. He joined her on the sofa. "Do you like it?" he asked her, for want of anything better.

"I love it." She took a long deep breath. "Lilac!" she said. "Nice. Where is everyone?"

"Richard is in the garden with Alex." He relaxed against the cushions with her. "Alex is my uncle, but he thinks 'uncle' sound too old."

She smiled again. "That's cool."

"Yes," he agreed. "Cool." He liked the way people used that word. "Do you want to see my room?"

She gave him a look which his did not understand, but it was more of a smile than anything else. "Sure." She noticed how the bannister was so smooth. The carpets so thick. The door catches so polished. "Have you got servants?"

"No." He was going to say how he had used have, but then remembered.

She sat on the edge of his bed. He joined her. It was another moment he wanted to freeze. "It's a nice room," she said. "No TV? Wow. Or is it hidden.?"

He shrugged "No TV."

"Oh yeah, I remember, you said you don't have one."

"We have one in the main room."

"Cool." She scanned the poster on his wall. "You're really into history and Kings and stuff, aren't you. I don't know much about my family's history, where we were before we came to England. I mean my non English side." She looked at him. "My white side. I guess your family have always been English, and white."

"I think so," he said. "And I like your black side. But you're not really black; more like golden brown. You're beautiful, inside and out, no matter what colour you are."

She gazed at him. "Wow! Thank." She kissed him lightly.

He felt himself blush. It made her smile again. He laughed a bit, then he brushed her hair. Then he kissed her. They kissed each other. They hugged while they kissed. Then they broke off and were silent for a moment. When she broke the silence, she just said, "Wow!"

"What?" he asked.

"You kiss good."

"Oh." He did not blush but he was too surprised to say more.

They linked arms. She studied the picture of British monarchs again. "That's Richard the third," she said. "I read about him in history when they did that re-burial. I think he's my least favourite. The one before him was called Edward. He died so young, only 12 ... or he was only King for a short while? It doesn't make it clear." She saw that he looked like he was concentrating on something. "Are you alright?"

He nodded.

"He was your age, and you are called Edward. That's kinda sad."

He looked at her. He wanted to tell her, but how could she believe him. He forced a smile. "I think he would have liked you."

"If he was like you, I would have liked him."

He enjoyed the touch of her hand on his. "What is your room like, in your house?"

"Cluttered." She even looked beautiful when she was embarrassed. "I can't take you there because my dad is kinda strict on that kinda thing. You know, boys in my room. But, hey, wait." She took out her mobile and found her photos. "This is one of me and Shelley in my room. A mess, huh?" She clicked through a few photos and then put her phone away. "The others are just rubbish," she laughed.

There were sounds from the house. Richard playing with Arthur. Alex filling the kettle. It seemed so normal, like it wasn't Edward's first full day in 2016. He felt a sudden swell of emotion. He swallowed it back but gripped her hand tighter. She noticed, of course. She leaned against him, feeling that he need it. "Edward …?"

He did not respond immediately but then asked, "What?"

"You haven't asked about the girl I met at the park. The one called Milly."

"I don't know any girls here apart from you, Shelley and Michelle. "

"She said you know a couple of guys called Ralph and Robert."

The names seemed to echo hollowly within him. He remembered the purple mist and the glimpse of Sir Ralph amid the shouting and fiery torches. It had been like a weird dream. Now he looked at Amber and had her repeat the names, to be sure he hadn't misheard. She gave him Milly's number.

Edward looked out of the window. Two loyal knights were out there, somewhere, searching for him. But then the doubts emerged. Was it likely that they would make themselves known to a girl from the new world? Would they not be too careful for that? But then, the hopes resurface. They were resourceful knights who would do anything necessary to achieve their aim. He pictured them, full armour, riding, swords in hand, through the streets of London, coming to his aid. Then he saw himself in the mirror and he knew that reality would not be the same.

He felt a charge of new power. New faith. New purpose. He knew it was just a reaction, but he had new hope. He looked at Amber, looking at him, and he kissed her fully. Then he held onto her, hugged her close. "I love you," he told her.

She loosened her grip with him. "What?"

"I Love you," he repeated. "No matter what happens. I love you."

She searched his eyes. "No matter what happens? What do you mean?"

He let her go and composed himself. Suddenly, he did not know what he meant. The boy who yearned to be a man, was not a man yet. Words had come which he was not ready for. "I'm sorry," he said softly.

"For what?" She smiled at him. "You said you love me."

"I do!"

"I think I do too ... but,"

"But?"

"What's that got to go with those guys?"

"Oh." He so wanted to tell her, but maybe it was too early. "Can I tell you later? It's a long, and strange story."

"Sure." She brushed his hair and admired it. "Whenever you are ready."

"Why are you so nice?"

They hugged again but more gently, tenderly. "Maybe because you are," she said.

Edward was wondering why he was not rushing to tell Richard about the knights. Why was he still in his room instead of phoning Milly? Was that what love did? Did it make all other emotions redundant? He was comfortable with Amber. He could have stayed in her arms forever. He wanted to melt into her. He wished his love for her could erase all the bad stuff he had experienced over the last few days.

Eventually, he let her go again. The boy was still a King, even if he no longer had a kingdom; he still had honour and responsibilities. He had to tell Richard. He had to connect with the knights. If the wizard was still at large, Edward knew that he, with his knights, had to see that he caused no further damage.

It all seemed less daunting now that his knights were in the same realm. He looked at the image of his father on the poster. He had seen that painting before. It did not look much like his father. His own was bad enough. The only thing the artist has got right was his blonde hair. He frowned at the image of his uncle. Maybe he could not change history, but he could still try to make his father proud of him, and bring honour to the house of York.

ख़

The 'rozzers' had poked their noses around the area where the knights had encountered Lance, but there was nothing to see or keep their interest. It was in a CCTV dark spot, so they went away again. The boy with the slingshot had kept Ralph and Robert posted. The old man was still with them in the building, as was the large raggedly man. Neither offered their names, so the knight's did not ask.

Lucas offered no more help and kept insisting they let him leave, but he seemed too timid to try to escape. Lance recovered but found that he was tied tightly to a post. The large raggedly man was guarding the doorway, rolling a cigarette. Robert called the boy over to him."

"Is there anywhere nearby where I can buy coffee?"

The boy shrugged. "Yeah."

"Go get some of them white cups full we can share."

"You kidding? Lump a tray of coffee down 'ere?" said the boy. "You want everyone to know you're up 'ere? Better get a flask and fill it, that's best way."

"Then do that then."

"What did your last slave die of?"

Robert met the boy's stare. "I ate him."

The boy sighed. "Yeh yeh!" He held up a hand to the knight. "Dosh."

Robert remembered the way Megan had called money 'dosh' so he handed over a note. The boy waited. Robert looked at him. "What?"

"More!"

"For what?"

"Flask. Coffee. Burger and tip."

Ralph laughed. "That young one will go far."

Robert handed over another note, and the boy sped off on his errand. Lance had another attempt to free himself from the post, but he was stuck fast. "What do you plan to do?" he asked. "You can't exactly keep me here for ever, and you won't get anything off me."

"We can keep you here for as long as it takes," Ralph told him. "We have nowhere else to go. We are long dead, remember."

"You are not dead," said Lance. "You can get on with your life here."

"We are knights sworn to serve our King," said Robert. "Only he can release us from our duty. Tell us where he is, and you may be freed. If not, you can stay here and rot."

The old man tittered.

Lance gave a half laugh. "Two things with that. At some point, someone will come in here. And, secondly, pretty soon this place may no longer exist."

"Meaning?" asked Ralph.

"You'll have to work that bit out for yourselves." He glanced at Robert. "You can knock me out as often as you like, it won't change a thing."

The old man started to speak but then, as quickly, lost his train of thought.

"So, it's a matter of time? Again," asked Ralph.

The old man tittered again, and clapped. "That's right!"

"Everything is a matter of time," said Lance. "The secret it …"

The knights both knew Lance had stopped himself from saying something crucial. Robert drew closer to him. "You might as well say it. Whatever you had planned, it's going to happen without you. What is the point of dying when you can so easily do something to make sure you stay alive?"

"I don't think he cares," said Ralph.

"I don't," said Lance.

Ralph beckoned to the large raggedly man who approached them slowly. "Take this piece of dung and toss him off the roof," said Ralph. "He wants to die anyway."

Lance struggled as he was unstrapped from the post and hoisted upwards. "You won't do this," he protested. "You are honourable knights. You don't commit cold murder."

Ralph shrugged. "As you said, we are dying anyway. We cannot find our King. Life has lost it's purpose."

"Bluff," called Lance as the large raggedly man carried him out. "All bluff!"

The old man watched with a mixture of wonder and concern. "He is right," he said, "You can't just kill him."

They could hear Lance still protesting as he was taken to the roof. There were plenty people in the street. Lance would make quite a bang as he landed. The police would be called. The knights would have to fight them. It would be a dishonourable ending to two former knights of the realm. But life is always more precious than you imagine, especially when you realise it is at it's bitter end.

Lance was nearly as his last gasp then he succumbed. The large raggedly man brought him back down in silence and dumped him in front of Ralph. "He promised me I would be safe no matter what happens," moaned Lance. "It would never come to this."

"Who is he?" asked Ralph. "Is he a wizard?"

"Wizard?" Lance sighed. "I suppose he would seem that way to people from your era. He's just a man, but he has a way of controlling time. I don't know how, he just does."

"If I was not living the story," said Robert. "I would refuse to believe it."

"Yes," agreed Ralph. "But here we are? How can we find this man? What name does he use?"

Lance laughed for a few seconds. "He calls himself Wolf, but I doubt it's his real name. I don't know what era he's from originally, or how often he has played with time. I just know he uses people, like he used me. I don't know how you will find him."

"How did you talk to him?" asked Robert. "With one of those speaking boxes?"

"I met him the first time, but all the other times he has left a message on my phone." Lance handed his phone to Ralph. "But he might know, now, that you have turned me."

"What is his intention regarding Edward?" asked Ralph.

"I don't know everything. He said he doesn't intend to harm the boy, but he must want something." Lance looked at Ralph. "He knows where the boy is. He will make his move soon."

∽

It did not surprise Edward when Milly had said she had no number for the knights. She would pass on his number then she next saw them. It had been a strange and awkward conversation. Edward would have preferred to have seen her face to face. He could not get a good picture of her over a phone, but she seemed pleasant enough. She had also seemed quite excited, which he saw as a good sign. Evil people don't tend to get excited so easily.

Richard was still buzzing from the prospect of seeing the knights again. He, too, felt a surge of new hope and energy. Even if they had to stay in this new England, they were no longer alone. He sat on the front doorstep, aware that the knights would not be arriving yet, but taking a moment to reflect.

He could hear Arthur inside, grumbling and moving about by the door. He was about to let the dog out when he saw John casually coming along the road. John stopped and leaned at the gate. "Hi," he said.

Richard joined to him. "Hello. I saw you talking to my brother earlier."

"Yeah, we chatted a bit. What are you doing?"

"Nothing," shrugged Richard.

"I'm not doing anything either." John jerked when he heard Arthur bark again. "What's wrong with your dog? He doesn't usually bark at people."

"Not sure," said Richard. He turned as Alex came out from the house. Arthur dodged past Alex and leaped at the gate, barking at John. The boy backed off.

Alex held on to Arthur and forced him back into the house. "I'm sorry about that," Alex apologised to John. "He seems to be out of sorts today." He turned to Richard. "Dad's seeing the doctor today, so we'll go a bit later than planned. Unless they call me and say he can come home."

"I hope he does come home," said Richard.

"Want to hang out for a bit?" John asked Richard. "Just round here, the park and stuff."

Richard glanced at Alex who put a hand on the young prince's shoulder. "If you want to," said Alex, carefully. "But remember you need to take things slowly for a while."

"I will," promised Richard.

"Try not to be more than hour."

Richard considered that. "How will I know?"

"How do you normally tell the time?"

"People tell me if I'm needed somewhere," said Richard. "I've never really had to think about it."

"I've got a watch on," said John. "So I'll tell him when it's time."

"Okay, have fun." Alex was not sure if it was a good idea, but Richard had been confined enough lately. He should have some freedom, and it was good if the boy was making a local friend. He watched as the boys crossed the road to the gardens.

They sat on one of the benches and chatted for a while. John had a relaxed manner about him. He did not even question when Richard failed to understand some of the things he said. The squirrels kept them entertained for a few minutes.

John pointed out the blocks of flats just around the corner. "That's where I live. You wanna go see?"

Richard hesitated. "I said I won't go far."

"It's not far!" John steered him on that direction. "And you only said you'd be an hour. It won't take us that long."

Richard had not ventured far in his new neighbourhood, apart from the trip to the hospital. The chance to explore was not something he normally missed. He smiled as a squirrel stepped onto his foot. It was a splendid Summer day. He looked along to the house, then at the flats. "Alright," he said.

John led the way through a pedestrian area, chatting away quite cheerfully. There were not many people; just a couple of women talking about the price of butter. A gateway led to a flight of stairs. John fished around in his pocket and found his key.

To Richard's surprise, the flat was unfurnished. "Why is this place so empty?" he asked.

"It's not our main home," John admitted. "This is down for repairs and decorating, but it's a place to hang about in and there's something I want to show you." He opened the far door and pointed bars on the window. The glass was bubbled as though it was a bathroom but, a part from that, it was just a room. "A mad guy used to live here. They locked him up in this room. Then they forgot about him and he starved to death."

Richard was doubtful. "Is that true?"

"Sure," said John. "You can see out the window, but only if you get close to the glass. People outside can't see in, unless they get a ladder."

Richard checked to see that was the case. The hole was quite small but he could still see most of the road when he pushed his face against the window.

"Do you believe in ghosts?" John asked him.

"Why?"

"Cos this place is haunted." John smiled his most terrifying smile.

"Oh, I don't believe you," said Richard. "You are just trying to scare me."

John looked at him. "Actually, I saw two ghosts today."

"Where?"

"Just by your house."

Richard suddenly had an uncomfortable feeling. "Not true," he said.

"There's one in this room right now." John was looking straight at him. "He's the ghost of a prince. Same name as yours. Funny that, innit."

"I'm going!" said Richard, but John pushed him back. The prince stumbled. "Hey!"

"You're going nowhere, yet." John quickly grabbed the door and, smiling cheekily, stepped through and slammed it close behind him.

Richard heard the key turn. He banged on the lever. "Hey! Let me out."

"Can't," sniggered John through the slit. "You don't exist. You're a phantom."

"DUNG HEAP!"

"Get out of this tower," challenged John. "I got to go. See yah."

Richard heard the main door close. He banged on the lever a few more times, then, remembering the story of the mad man, felt a touch of panic. He crossed to the window and looked through the hole to see John outside, looking up and smiling. John gave a quick, dramatic wave and ran away.

"Dung Heap!" repeated Richard. He kicked the wall and then flopped against it. He had a sudden suspicion that John may have been the wizard from the mist. Maybe he could shape shift somehow.

Why had he done any of this? What was the point? It was obviously not just a childish prank. Was he really going to be trapped alone in this room until he died? No. He was not going to let that happen.

◅

"Come on," urged the slingshot boy, pushing the knights and the rest of the party towards the stairs.

"Rozzers! I told you they'd be back."

The large raggedly man held his ground. "I ain't ever run from Rozzers, and I don't intend to start now."

"Nor I," said the old man.

"You stay here then," The boy turned to the others. "They are just around the corner, asking questions, and they'll be here in no time, so scram."

"I'm normally of their mind," said Ralph. "But we cannot afford to waste time. We have important things to do."

"Whatever," said the boy. "You guys follow me." He led the way through an alley which came out by a railway bridge. Lucas took the opportunity to run in the opposite direction. The boy looked at Robert. "Want me to get after him?"

"No," Robert gazed at the disappearing figure. "Let the rat go. He's of no use to us." He looked at Lance. "Are you going to run too?"

Lance shook his head. "There's no point. In a few hours it will be all over."

"Not if we can prevent that," said Ralph.

"What will be over?" asked the boy. He suddenly realised they had stopped, and he urged them on again. "Come on, this street it riddled with cameras. Just try go casual."

They walked under the bridge and turned along a narrow road which took them back under another bridge. The boy knew the area well. He led them through several dark places. Had them wait in aa old yard until he was convinced it was safe for them to emerge. Then came back onto the main road under yet another wide, rumbling, railway bridge.

"You could sell your services as a guide," Ralph told him.

The boy grinned. "I'll give you the bill later."

"I suspect you would be a skilled thief," said Robert.

"I ain't never took anything from people who didn't deserve it," shrugged the boy.

"What is your name?" asked Ralph.

The boy looked at him. "I ain't asked yours, so you don't need to know mine."

"Spoken like a true spy," winked Robert.

The boy ignored the bait. "Where do you want to head for?"

"Which way to a place called Weavers Fields?"

"Cor," the boy stopped to think. "If you don't want to get a bus then just stick with me. But I never got you that coffee so we should tank up before we go that way." He looked up at the knights. "You can call me Kit."

"Is that your actual name?" asked Robert.

"It's my name, take it or leave it."

"I heard that name before," said Ralph. "Yesterday, Milly mentioned it. You were keeping the Rozzers busy."

Kit shrugged. "I get around." He led them to a coffee bar where they 'tanked up'.

"How do you know the old man?" asked Ralph.

Kit took a bite of biscuit and munched before replying. "Just though Milly and Megan. Anyway, you tell me your names now."

"Ralph and Robert," said Ralph.

Kit smiled eyed Lance. "And you're not nice. A bit of a toe-rag, so I don't care what your name it. But now you tell us what you meant by 'it will all be over'".

"I don't care to tell you anything," Lance told him. "You're the kind of scumbag the world never needed to start with."

Kit threw his coke over Lance. Robert got between them. "Neither of you are perfect, but we have a quest which both of you are part of now. No fighting amongst ourselves. The road leads to defeat."

"Quest?" asked Kit.

Lance explained it to the boy. "Didn't you know? These guys are medieval knights trying to find the princes in the tower?"

Kit looked from one knight to the other, then at Lance. "Yeah? Well it's better than being a lying toe-rag."

"Enough!" Robert put a hand on Kit but the boy pushed it off him.

"Medieval knights!" Kit studied Robert. "Pull the other one, it rings dixie. Where's your time machine?"

"Whether or not we are knights," Ralph told him." We do have a quest. We need your help. Can we count on you?"

Kit backed away from them, sensing something both disturbing and enticing. The hairs on the back of his neck were doing a tango. He looked at Ralph. "I'm not a little kid!"

"I see that," said the knight.

"I don't just believe any old tripe."

"I can see that too."

Kit saw the difference between the knights and Lance. Part of him wanted to walk away but, mostly, he was intrigued. He did not feel threatened by the knights. The remaining child within him recognised the quality that all knights in stories possessed. If these were not knights, then they at least believed themselves to be knights. But it was more than that. He looked deep into their eyes, and he knew.

"Get me another coke and I'm with you," he said "But lose him. He'll only betray you." He pointed to Lance.

Robert considered Lance for a moment. Was there any point in keeping him with them? If it was true that time was so short, and if he had really become useless to both sides, they should just release him.

"Suits me," said Lance. "But, like I said ..."

"It will all be over," echoed Kit. "Yeah, yeah."

Robert put a hand on Kit's shoulder, but it was not pushed away this time. He looked at Lance. "I would ask for your word, but you are without honour. If I had not given my word, I would have killed you by now."

Lance flinched.

"I'll fix him so he don't say nothing," said Kit. "I'll just say he touched me, then he'll get locked up."

Robert slightly tightened his grip on the boy's shoulder. "There'll be no lies or falsehoods, or threats. We serve the side of good." He slackened his grip again. "Do you understand, boy?"

"My name is Kit. But, yes."

Robert turned his attention back to Lance. "Go," he ordered. "Do not get in our way again and you shall live in peace. If you do anything to bring harm to King Edward, or Prince Richard, or this good friend, I shall forget my promise and end your life."

Lance was about to repeat his claim that 'it will all be over' but changed his mind and walked quickly along the road. The knights, and Kit, watched him leave. The boy looked at Robert's hand on his shoulder, then at the knight's face.

"Why did you call me a good friend?" he asked. "You hardly know me."

Robert pressed the boy's hand. "You could have walked away, but here you are. You have some doubts, but there is good inside of you. I recognise that good. And you have courage."

Kit gave a crooked smile. "A bit mushy, but thanks man."

The trio made their way towards Weavers Field, taking whichever route Kit was the most direct. They all were aware that their journey would be recorded in places but, if they stayed casual, it would hardly be noticed among the crowds of others.

Ralph felt a touch of excitement at the thought of seeing Milly again, but only a fraction compared to the way he had felt earlier. Maybe the emotion sickness was wearing off. It was being replaced by a stronger determination to finish the quest.

Gradually, the knights began to see familiar buildings, then the railings around Weavers Fields. They could hear music from a folk band performing not far from the west gate. Kit brought a mobile from his pocket and punched numbers.

"I didn't know you had one of those things," said Robert.

"I didn't," said Kit. "I nicked it off Lance." He stopped to listen to a voice in his ear. "Milly. Hey, it's me Kit ... yep, they're here, where are you? ... okay cool ... yeah, I see you." He waved as Milly and Megan came into view.

Ralph thought that Milly, somehow, looked younger, but she was still very attractive. He smiled at her and she blushed. She dared to touch his hand. "I spoke to Edward," she told him, quite excitedly. "He sounds very nice. Very together."

He admired her enthusiasm. "Of course," he said. "He is a King!"

She giggled slightly. "If you say so," She said.

∽

Richard was late. Edward and Amber agreed to look around the park area. Amber knew it well because one of her aunts used to live just beyond it. Alex took Arthur to check around the flats. They were hoping that Milly and the knights would follow up.

Edward was a bit annoyed with his brother for going exploring at a crucial time, but he was also concerned. He had figured that Arthur, like most dogs, had good senses and had a good reason for barking. Something was not right.

The park was of similar size to Weavers Fields. Boys were playing football near the main entrance. Various people were enjoying the sun. Edward and Amber searched the faces but Richard's current clothing was not as eye catching as his 1483 costume. It would only be his hair style that gave him away.

Edward saw a glimpse of a familiar figure and he set off in pursuit of a boy who looked like John. The boy was running and, soon, ducked behind a bush. Edward caught up to him and found him crouching out of sight. He swung him around, but it was not John.

"Hey, what you doing?" asked the boy. "Push off!"

Edward apologised. It was unlikely that Richard or John was in the park at all. It was more likely that they were in the flats, and Alex would find them first.

"If you guys had your own phones," said Amber. "Life would be so much easier."

"Didn't Alex give you his number?" asked Edward.

"Yes, but I mean so that you can find Richard. All you'd need to do would be call him."

Edward shrugged. "But Richard hasn't got a phone. That's just the way it is." He froze. "Wait! That's John." He set off in pursuit again.

John saw him, grinned, and began running. He was fast. He soon left the other behind. Then he stopped, waited for them, changed direction and began running again. He was playing with them, luring them one way, then another, always smiling or laughing.

"It's cat and mouse," said Amber. "My brother does that all the time. No point in just running after him when he's this quick."

Edward agreed and beckoned John to come to them. He was not too surprised when all John did in response was invite them to come to him. "Little rat!" grumbled Edward. He called to John, "Where is Richard?"

John just shrugged and spread his hands.

"I bet Richard went home," said Amber.

Edward was not sure. He watched as John slowly backed away, smiling, challenging them. There was something about his manner. Something not quite playful. He had seen it before. He shook his head. "I don't think Richard went home."

"Why not?"

"Just a feeling." Edward began to walk towards John, who kept just the same distance from the young King, always checking behind him. They covered quite a lot of ground and were soon at the far side of the park.

"Why doesn't the little beast say anything?" asked Amber.

"He's trying to vex us."

"It's working!"

"You know this area," said Edward. "What lies beyond this road, the way he is leading us?"

"It in my aunt's old district. It's not the best place. That's why she moved." Amber saw the way John was eyeing her. "That kid is kinda creepy. Can't we just turn back. He's just doing this to be a pain."

Edward took her had in his and pressed it. "You can go if you want," he said, gently. "I think it's just me he wants."

"Wants?" She held his hand firmly. "What do you mean?"

"I'm not sure," he admitted. "But I've felt that something was going to happen. Something had to, to give meaning to everything."

She looked at him in silence. Something was going to happen? To him? She felt a chill, and a tingling. She remembered his costume. His different way of talking. The way she felt when they had kissed. His face when she had talked about the old Kings. What was going to happen?

She stopped walking. He turned and she saw, in his face, something haunting, lonely, afraid but determined. He looked at her and nodded understanding. She owed him nothing. She could just walk away. Her heart ached. She did owe him something, even in just a day, she owed him her friendship and ... yes, love. She caught up with him again.

He gazed at her. "You don't have to come."

She took his hand. "Yes I do."

Edward remembered the way he waited, in those long uncertain days, in the tower. The dreams. Richard in a cage of bones. This new London so unlike his old one. He did not belong, even though he had started to believe he could, in time. He thought about that word, 'Time'. He had no idea what the next few moments would bring. Still he wondered why? Was this just a final torture before the ultimate end?

They turned another corner and followed a street of terraced houses until they reached a shorter road flanked by a couple of old work yards. John led them into one of the yards where he eyed Amber again. She stared back at him. He pushed open a door and held it for them.

"What's in here?" asked Edward.

"Answers," he said, simply.

Edward let go of Amber's hand. "I have a bad feeling about this," he told her. "I don't think you should be here."

She took his hand again. "Neither should you. I don't like this place, and I don't like him." She glared at John again.

He stuck his thumb out at her.

Edward was surprised that he was not shaking as he looked at her. Some strange calm had come upon him. He kissed her softly. "Please go home."

She shook her head. "Not without you."

"I think they have Richard," he said.

"I think I guessed that," she said. "And I think I don't want you to be alone. Girls can be brave too, you know."

Edward smiled despite the circumstances. They both stepped into an old warehouse. It had a musty smell. John opened another door, to an office, and went to stand beside a man who Edward recognised.

"It's you!" The young King confronted the wizard. "I should have known."

"Yes, you should have," said the man. "In fact, you did, deep down, didn't you? You're quite an intelligence boy. That's why you still live."

"What do you mean?"

"They were going to kill you, and your brother. Murder you!" The wizard relaxed on a chair. "I could not let that happen. You are too valuable to my plans." He glanced at Amber. "Sit down my dear. I mean you no harm."

She remained standing, anyway. "Who are you? What's going on?"

The wizard smiled. "My name would mean nothing to you, but I am called Daren Wolf. Soon to be King Daren of England." He put a hand on John. "And this is my son, soon to be Prince John."

Edward huffed. "A wizard who desired to be a King. Utter nonsense! If magic could make you a king, you would not need me, or even my wicked uncle."

Daren kept the same soft smile. "I am no wizard," he admitted. "To someone like you, even in this modern age, it may seem that way, but magic has nothing to do with it. It's a form of science!"

"It's wrong," said Edward. "Whatever name you give it. You have meddled with things that should be left alone."

"You would rather be dead?" Daren gazed at him. "That your brother be dead? I can offer you a second chance."

"To help you to become King in my stead?" Edward met his gaze. "I will never do that. And my people would never follow you."

"They would, if you told them to."

"And why should I ever do that?"

Daren relaxed again. "To save your brother, for one reason."

"What have you done with him?"

"Oh, he's safe." Daren sat forward and leaned towards Edward. "I offer a deal. You can keep your castle in Ludlow. Live there with your mother, sisters, brother," he looked at Amber. "Even your chosen bride. You can be King of Wales. I have no interest in that place. You know that you are too young to be an effective King of England. That's how you lost the throne."

Amber sat down suddenly. She looked at Edward, digesting the reality. "So ... you are THAT Edward. The one who didn't stay King for very long. Oh, my ... "

"I'm sorry," said Edward. "I wanted to tell you, but ..."

"You really were King of England!"

Edward sat beside her. "Not quite," he said. "My uncle stole my throne and had me locked up in the tower." He touched her finger and she accepted the gesture. Edward looked back at Daren. "They might not have murdered us. My army was coming to my aid."

"I told you, your army was in tatters," said Daren. "Most of those loyal to you were either dead, under arrest or in flight. Your uncle was quite convincing when he spoke to parliament, but so long as you, or your brother, still lived, there was a chance of revolt. In fact, three rebels came too close to success for my liking. They were intercepted, by my gullible followers, and used as test subjects for time flight. "

"But you still need Edward," said Amber.

"Yes," Edward stepped in. "Because he is not of noble blood, and he had no honour. Though he might be able to take the throne by force, he would never be trusted and might be murdered in the night."

"That's pretty much it," admitted Daren. "But with the blessing of Edward, if he chooses to agree with my plan, I can lead England to a better future."

Edward sighed. "It still would not happen without an army."

Daren smiled. "That was while you were a prisoner in the tower. Now you will be free to muster a viable force. Imagine the change that would make. But, forget honour and nobility. Power is more important."

"You are wrong," argued Edward. "It is about honour. Doing the right thing for your country. A King lives to serve the people. My father taught me that."

"Your father became King by beating his enemies," said Daren.

"There was more to it than that," said Edward. "And my father was a man of peace. He brought peace between England and France. Also between England and Scotland. He was a fair and just and popular."

"And he died." He took John by the arm and moved towards the door. "As all people must. He left a child with the burden of state, and all that he worked for was destroyed because he was too weak to plan differently."

"Not all," said Edward.

"Now you have the chance to claw some of your father's reputation back from the brink. And I shall start a new regime with my own son. A new dawn for England." Daren opened the door. "I shall leave you to think about it for a while."

"How do I know Richard is safe?" asked Edward. "I want to see him."

Daren nodded. "You will see him. Later." He closed the door behind him, and they could hear the key turning.

Amber stared at the door lever, emotions clashing, turning inside her. She looked at Edward. She let go of him. Backed away from him. Came back to him. She put her head in her hands. "This is real? This is happening? I can't believe it." She tried the door. Banged on it, then remembered her mobile. "I'm calling the police!"

There was no signal.

Edward went to her but she backed off again. He could tell that her mind was in turmoil. She turned to him. Slapped him, then regretted it and hugged on to him. "I'm so sorry. Oh god I am." She was weeping. "What are they going to do with us?"

He was struggling himself, to hold on; to make some kind of sense of everything. He brushed a tear from her cheek. "They won't hurt us. They need me too much."

"But they don't need me!" she groaned.

He knew she was right. And they knew he loved her. Suddenly he understood love; what it meant. He was twelve, almost thirteen, and he loved Amber more than anything, or anyone, he had ever known. She was beautiful, caring, understanding and did not deserve this. With both love and Kingship comes great responsibility. He was twelve! Was he strong enough to handle so much?

"I won't let them hurt you," he promised. The words were easy, but could he live up to them?

For The People

There was a dead moth in the corner. It could have been dead for ages. Richard had prodded it several times to relieve the monotony of his imprisonment. The door was too solid and the window too limited. He felt hollow and wretched but he still refused to cry.

A sound in the building caught his attention. He listened carefully, then pressed himself against the door. Someone was coming! Not John. Too heavy. He heard footstep halt, then the key being turned. He backed away from the door as it opened and a man came in carrying a collection of clothes.

The man tossed the clothes to Richard. "Put these on."

Richard examining the clothing. It was not unlike the stuff he used to wear, and seemed to be about the right size. "What for?"

The man also handed him a carton drink and a sausage roll. "You want to go home, don't you?"

"Where is my brother?"

"Your brother is safe. Don't worry about him."

Richard noted that the door was still ajar. He had heard too many lies and false promises to just take the man's word. "Take me to him now," he ordered.

The man laughed. "You're not a prince here. Get changed."

Richard threw the clothes and food at the man and bolted for the door. The key was gone but he banged the door on his captor and headed for the stairs. He should have known that it would not be so easy. A second man caught him half way down the stairs. Then the first came down and, together, they wrestled the wildly wriggling prince back towards the room. The bitter end of Richard's emotions took over. He landed a vicious kick in the first man's groin, sending him flying. The other was surprised by the boy's determination but held on until something pounced on him.

Richard landed, stunned, against the bannister, his clothing messed up and pain in his chest. He saw what looked like a whirlwind, and heard the man crying out, with intermittent growling, as the second man tumbled down the stairwell. The first man, slightly recovered, grabbed Richard again. The prince clung to the bannister, prepared to be beaten, but then this fight was over.

The pistol aimed at the villain had Alex on the end. "Back up to the room," Alex ordered the man. "And hand over the key."

Arthur reappeared and growled as the door was locked. Alex picked up the young prince who clung on to him silently. Richard was slightly in shock so they made their way to the ground floor and outside where the air was fresh. The second villain had scooted.

"How did you find me?" asked Richard in a half daze.

Alex put a soothing hand on the boy. "When I feel lost, I follow the dog. Arthur found you."

Alex carried Richard who was light in his arms. Arthur, alert and protective, flanked them all the way home, but issued a warning as strangers approached. Alex stopped warily and Richard, sensing his uncertainty, turned to view the oncomers.

Richard stiffened. He looked at one of them in particular, and then recognition dawned. He freed himself and ran to his trainer, his hero, his friend. "Sir Ralph!" he cried, tears melting on his cheeks. "Sir Ralph! Sir Ralph!" He climbed on the knight's chest and hugged his neck.

Robert shook the hand of Alex. "So you have been their champion. Well met!" He looked at the way Richard was hugging Ralph. "Where is our King?"

Alex told the story as best he could, ending with the man locked in the flat. Robert cursed silently. "You must take me to the captive. I shall make him talk or he will wish he was dead."

Kit saw the pistol poking out from Alex's pocket. "Is that a real gun?" he asked.

Alex remembered it and showed it. "No. It's a fake. I hoped the guy would not notice that, and he didn't. Good thing too. I'm not much of a fighter."

Robert patted him at the back. "You did well enough! Come, let us confront this weasel."

"I'll come with you guys," said Kit.

"It might not be pretty," warned Robert.

Kit shrugged. "Neither am I," he grinned. "Besides, I know this area good. I was born in the shadow of The Tower. Once he spills his guts, I can scout ahead of you."

Robert nodded. "There is much wisdom in your thinking."

Ralph accepted the house key off Alex and he watched the go along the road towards the flats. Arthur gave a quick bark and followed them. Milly and Megan felt a bit redundant as they accompanied Ralph into the house, so they found the kettle and made tea. Ralph settled Richard on the sofa.

"How do you feel, Your Highness?"

Richard smiled at the sound of the title but was more pleased to be in the comfortable hands of a loyal knight. His chest still hurt from his tussle, and he was worried about Edward, but the arrival of the two knights felt like the arrival of an army. "Better," he said.

"I regret that we did not arrive sooner," said Ralph. "But, as you can see, we found friends in this new world. We are still few, but we have the right spirit."

"Too true," said Megan, coming in with a tray and handing a cup to Richard. "Drink this slowly. It's hot."

Richard tested it carefully. It was sweet, and quite strong. He didn't know what it was, but it seemed to have a calming quality. "Thank you," he said.

Megan studied him. "So," he looked at Ralph. "This is one of the princes in the tower. He looks ... normal." She winked at Richard and he smiled. "A fine looking boy. He doesn't deserve what's happen to him. Nobody does."

Milly came in and sat near to Ralph. She considered the boy for a moment. "What's going to happen to him now?" It was more of a curious thought than a question.

Ralph squatted on the floor and brushed hair away from Richard's face. He met the boy's eyes, touched his brow, and wondered at the circumstances that had brought them to this place today. "Whatever happens, he will be safe. I vow that with my life."

৯

They had not been hugging all the time, but they were when they heard the key again. They did not break free from each other. Both turned to see Daren, and a man with a cut lip, come into the room. Daren placed a selection of clothes on a chair and looked at Edward.

"Ah!" He smiled. "Young love! It's good that you have a suiter. Quite fortunate, actually." He touched Amber's hair and she pulled away from him. He laughed. "Yes. That will work out very well."

"Leave her alone," Edward warned him. "She's got nothing to do with this."

"Ah, but you are wrong. She, now, has everything to do with it." He grabbed Amber to him and held her tight. When Edward responded, the man with the cut lip held him fast. Daren watched him with relish. "Yes, you love her. You would die for her, and after only one day together. That's what I call true love. But would you kill for her?"

Edward struggled against his captor. "I'd kill you!" he said.

Daren laughed again, and pushed Amber aside. "I have no wish to hurt either of you. I have already told you that, but time is getting short now." He motioned for Edward top be released. "That brat of a brother of yours escaped."

Edward could not resist a smile of satisfaction.

"It seems that your ragtag of followers have rescued him. But," Daren held up a hand. "As it happens, I don't really need him anyway. I had doubts about whether your chosen lady would fit in 1483 culture, not as more than a slave, but, you have the right charm, and with all the changes I will bring, Britain will be an entirely different place."

"You talk too much," said Edward.

Another laugh from Daren. "You might be right." He pointed to the clothing. "Dress fit for a young King. You are going back to 1483, within the hour. Either freely, or in chains. You choose."

"You won't win any friends with me in chains," said Edward.

"Oh, I'll take the chains off once we are there. When it is too late to change anything that matters." Daren gently took hold of Amber's hand. "Come my dear. I have dress fit for a queen in another room."

Edward took a few steps towards him but was stopped by Cut Lip. He felt almost powerless as he watched Amber being taken away. She looked afraid. He was shoved backwards as Cut Lip left the room and locked the door behind him.

He remembered Sir Ralph's advice, to never let hatred take control. That was hard advice to follow. Right then he wanted to kill Daren. Then he thought back to all those who had been killed, murdered, under order of his uncle, in a battle for power. If he gave in to hate, he would be no better. He wished that Sir Ralph was here now. He knew he was close, but he might as well be on the moon.

He started getting undressed. Now he missed the comfortable clothes of this new world. The old style clothes were finely made. Yes, fit for a King, in 1483. He remembered that night when he and Richard were getting dressed in The Tower, when they were taken in the cart to the ring of torches. How he had felt the cold threat of death. Had it really only been yesterday?

Edward pulled on the tunic and automatically felt for his crucifix. Yes, it had ripped from his neck that night. Now he wondered about Richard, but was pleased that his brother was safe. At least that was one small victory. He caught a flash memory of his fight with Tigger. Not a fight to the death, but he had given a good account of himself. Then Alex, the friend in disguise. And the good, faithful Miles.

He looked like a King again, but he felt small. Inadequate! Was he good enough to be King? He pictured his father, not perfect but noble and wise. What would his father do now? *"Do right by the people first, then for those you love most."* What people did Edward have? He was not King to the people of 2016. But, those he loves, Amber, Richard, Miles, Sir Ralph ... Alex. No, that's not all that his father had meant. The people! He was King of England. It did not matter that he was out of his own time frame. He had a duty to the people, even if they did not know who he was.

The key turned. Daren stepped in. "Good! You have changed. I see you have made the right decision."

"Where is Amber?" asked Edward.

"Safe," Daren assured him. "And I mean safe. I will not lose her the way I lost Richard."

"So you admit that Richard is lost to you."

Daren sighed. "You still don't understand." He sat on a chair. "When we go back to 1483, all that happens afterwards will be different from the history that this modern world knows. Richard, and all exists right now, will cease to exist. He truly will be lost."

Edward stared had at Daren then, realising that he was serious, he gasped despite himself. He tried to make sense of it, then found a straw to cling to. "That cannot be," he said. "You talk as thought you have travelled time before. My old servant lives now, in this time. He obviously did not cease to exist."

"I love the way people overuse the word 'obviously'. No, he did not," admitted Daren. "But, when I travelled time before, it was just for a short period, a few hours here and there, to help get things prepared for this ultimate journey. Not much of significance happened to change the course of history in those hours. But, in time, and with your help, many things can change."

For a brief moment, Edward felt sick. He gathered himself. This had to be stopped but, for now, he was alone. Was he ready to do battle, in any way, against this man with his strange control of time? This was no game. The stakes were extremely high. He was young and fit but he realised that he was sweating. He was terrified, but he had to swap that fear for determination.

He heard himself speaking more like in a dream. The courage was not his own, he thought. It could not be. For some reason he imagined his brother arguing with him to the contrary. He focused on his brother's faith in him. "I'll make an agreement with you," He defied the fear.

Daren looked interested. "Oh?"

"I'll go along with your plan if you beat me in combat."

Another laugh from Daren. "Combat? With a child?"

"I am a King!" announced Edward, proudly. "And I fight for my people, both now and in the past."

"Very commendable," said Daren. "But I would crush you."

"You need me," said Edward. "But if I win, you will abandon your plans and allow people to live in peace. You will no longer play games with time."

"If you win, you must kill me," said Daren. "I will never stop. Have you ever killed a man before? I have. It's an odd feeling, the first time, but it gets easier ... for me. You see, I don't fear death. I don't care about others. I don't care about honour, duty or any other that rubbish. If this was a story, I would be the bad guy, and you would be the good, but this is not a story. I don't even care about you. I only care about the power that you can give me. So, are you prepared to take a life?"

Edward felt suddenly small again. He slightly lowered his head and tried to control the raging panic within him.

Daren looked at him like he was nothing. "You have no hope of beating me in combat."

"Get some swords." The boy heard the words coming out from his mouth. It was very weird. His inner self, which Sir Ralph had often said would guide him, was taking over.

Daren looked at him and nodded. "We don't really have time for this, but it shouldn't take long. Then, as you agreed as a man of honour, you shall be all mine." He left to find swords.

Edward collapsed onto a chair and took deep breaths. He had proved himself capable in practice against boys of his own size. He was quick and agile. Sir Ralph had said that Edward was a worthy opponent, but he had never fought for real. Tigger was the closest he had come. He looked up as Amber came in accompanied by Cut Lip and John. She looked as beautiful as a Royal Bride in 1483 costume.

Daren followed and handed a sword to Edward. "You could always concede now," he said. "Save your beloved some heartache."

Edward rose to his feet and got the feel of the sword. He sensed Amber's concern and took strength from her eyes. "I love you," he told her, for all to hear. "I fight for England, truth, justice and you."

Daren grinned. He stripped off his tunic then turned to Edward. "Take off your tunic again," he said. "When we are done, you need to look your best." He waited while Edward got ready, then he stroked a bracelet before handing it to John.

The shirtless young King considered his own muscles compared to Daren's and wondered if this was another way that the man was trying to get a psychological advantage over the boy. Edward put the thought aside as Daren lunged at him, trying to take him by surprise. Edward dodged and evaded him. A chair was spent spinning. Amber shuddered. Daren lunged again and then tried for a swipe, but Edward's youth gave him the advantage.

Adrenaline fuelled the young King. He came at Daren with a fury of attacks that caught the villain by surprise, but Daren saw an opening and cut Edward's arm. The boy almost fell. Another hit from Daren and Edward could taste his own blood. He steadied himself just in time.

"Stop it," cried Amber.

Daren had the obvious experience. He was a skilled swordsman. Edward felt that he was fighting for his life, even though he knew it was not. He could quit, but there was too much at stake. He was holding his own, but struggling. He noticed that Daren was favouring his left side, so Edward dodged again and managed to slice a bit off Daren's ear.

There was a commotion outside, then the sound of the outer door breaking. Edward was just aware of Cut Lip leaving the room. Daren came at him again and flung the young King against another chair. "Yield," he demanding.

"No!" Shouted Edward. He fiercely fought back, ranging blows and slices against a retreating Daren. He saw the door flung open and felt the icy pain of Daren's sword plunging into his leg. He cried as Robert crashed in. The knight descended on Daren, dagger drawn, but Edward called out.

"Hold, Sir Robert." He as bleeding badly but he knew what he had to do. "I gave my word."

Robert stopped. "What? My King. No!"

Ralph stepped also. He looked at Edward's wound.

Daren shook his head. "You idiots and your sense of honour."

"It's not over yet," said Edward. "you don't get me until you have earned me." He resumed combat. If he gave in now, despite his injury, he would fail five hundred years of history and all the lives and achievements therein. He fought with what strength he had left. Daren knocked him down again, and pinned his good arm to the ground.

"You fought well, Edward," he breathed. "But it is over. Do yield now?"

Edward looked at Amber. The tears in her eyes. He looked at Sir Ralph, his trainer, and the loyal Sir Robert. He saw, for the first, Kit in the doorway. There was only one way to end this. He mustered all of his remaining strength and used his free hand to plunge his sword into Daren's chest.

The would-be ruler of history gave a quick jerk of surprise and flopped dead against the young King.

Edward stared in horror at what he had just done then he too collapsed.

Ralph, Robert and Amber all ran to Edward and dragged the dead non-wizard off him. Edward was breathing unsteady. Ralph ripped the young King's tights and tried to bandage the wounds, using Edward's tunic. He was proud of the boy but also ashamed that he might be too late to save him.

Amber could only look on, wiping the tears from her eyes. She was not sure if it was possible to fall in love in just a day, but she felt that she had. Edward was from a time five hundred years before she was born. With everything else, she believed that. She believed in him. Had she come so close to becoming a Queen? It was like a story book, but with a bitter twist.

She stared in disbelief as Daren's body began to fade into a purple mist. It soon disappeared altogether. She gingerly patted her foot against the space where Daren had been and looked at the others.

"Well," admitted Ralph. "That was unexpected."

"Indeed," agreed Robert.

Amber got down and held Edward's hand, tears still in her eyes. "He will be alright, won't he?" she asked. "Oh ..." Edward's wound was healing in front of them. His breathing levelled. Amber's tears fell on the boy's face and he opened his eyes. "I don't understand," she cried. "What's happening?"

The young King looked at her in a daze and checked himself. The pain was gone! The blood had gone! He held her as he tried to rise. He looked at the empty space. Had he been dreaming?

Ralph and Robert knelt and bowed their heads. This was strange, but much had been strange these past two days.

Edward touched their heads. "Get up, my Lords. I don't know what has just happened but I am still just me."

Kit approached them curiously. "You guys are so weird! That kid hopped it, by the way. I didn't know whether to stop him or what. He saw that bloke disappear and then legged it. What the heck happened to that dead guy anyway?"

Amber was more than slightly amazed. "That Daren told us that the boy was his son. Prince John. Why would a son just leave his father like that?"

Edward remembered the bracelet. He sat down to think through the day. Again he looked at the space left by Daren. Was the bracelet more than just jewellery? There was no way he could be certain but, yes, Amber was right. A son would not just leave a father's body, even if he felt his own life was in peril.

And what of Daren? Had Edward killed him, or was this more magic? Edward did not feel sick or at all ashamed, as he thought he would. Did that mean that he had not really killed Daren? Or was Daren never really alive in the first place?

Amber could not stop glancing at the place where Daren's body had been. It was forming a theory in her mind, but knew it would be difficult to explain it to Edward or the knights. She turned to Kit. "You know in computer games where you get killed so you just go back to the beginning and start again?"

"Uh-Huh," he nodded.

"Suppose it's a bit like that. Not totally, but a bit." She looked at the empty space again. "Suppose there was a wizard and an apprentice. If something happened to the wizard but he had cast a spell on something, like a bracelet, so that his apprentice could take it somewhere and make everything start all over."

Ralph caught the thread. "Like a special rock in a certain place." He turned to Robert. "The old man was saying something about that stone in the field where we first arrived."

"Indeed," remembered Robert.

Amber thought she was on something here, but ... "But, it can't be quite like that. Edward got well again when Daren disappeared, but Edward is still here."

"But John is not," joined Edward.

"And John has taken the bracelet with him." Said Amber. "Maybe to start the game over again."

"Cept," said Kit. "It's not a game. Wow! Do you guys do this kinda thing a lot?"

"Thankfully not," said Robert. "But we must waste no more time." He turned to Edward. "Your Majesty, with your permission, I will take our young scout directly to that field. If the boy returns there we can be heady."

Edward nodded agreement. He was feeling more settled now but still not up to running all the way to Weavers Fields. He watched them go and heard Kit asking Robert, "Why did you call that kid Your Majesty?" as they went out.

Ralph put a hand on Edward's shoulder. "How do you feel, My King?"

Edward relaxed on the chair still amazed but relieved that he was in one piece. "Is Richard truly alright?" he asked. "Is he safe and well?"

"He is." Ralph had a quick look outside the door to make sure that there were no threats. Cut Lip and another foe lay unconscious where they had landed from Robert's fist. They were not going anywhere soon. "His Highness is in the care of Alex who, I believe is trustworthy." He picked up one of the swords and judged it for weigh and balance.

Edward watched the knight, pleased to have him at his side. He felt small again, but secure. He still wondered at the effects the magic had on him. Twice in forty eight hours he had looked death in the face. Now he felt trapped between victory and uncertainty. "Stay with me, please, Sir Ralph." He said. "I value your presence."

Ralph nodded. "As you wish my King."

Edward was remembering Daren words with some sadness. "We can never go home," he said. "I know that now. All that we have seen, and all the people that we now know in this time, will be lost if we go back." He clutched to Amber's hand. "I shall never see my mother again, or my sisters."

"We cannot know for certain, surely," said Ralph.

Amber lay a hand on Edward cheek. "I could go to your time with you," she told him, a little uncertainly.

He half smiled at the gesture. "You would miss your family and end up hating me for bringing you there. It is a hard life compared to this one. That is obvious from just the short time I have been here." He brushed her hair. "I could not wish that on you. Plus, I am not sure that it would be possible."

"But you would be leaving so much behind too," she said. "If you stay here. Your mother. Your Kingdom."

Edward nodded. "Yes, but I know, or at least believe, that Darren was telling the truth that there is a way back in time, but life would begin again. If I was to go back, there is the possibility that I would lose my Kingdom anyway. I could go back and still be murdered. And you might not even be born. Daren was going to use his magic to gain power. Suppose we gain his power. The price would be too high. If we play with time, we shall be no better than he was." Edward brushed a sudden tear from his cheek. He looked at Ralph. "Am I truly your King?" He asked.

"For always," assured Ralph.

"Then, as your King I rule that none of us shall use whatever magic, or power, Daren possessed, no matter how right it may seem. Because it can never be right." He took a long breath. "I am sorry that you and Sir Robert have been trapped here also. I did not intend for any of this to happen."

Ralph nodded slowly, considering the consequences of not going back. "I would have liked to seen Adam again," he admitted. "But, other than he, I have no reason for regret. I swore to serve you, in this century or any other. With each campaign there was a chance I might not return, so I made arrangements that Adam inherit all that I have. No, I have no regrets."

Edward touched the knight's arm. "When this is resolved I shall no longer be your King."

"You will always be my King."

Edward shook his head. "No. England has a Queen now." He rose and took Ralph's hand on his. "I would like to be just your friend."

The knight nodded. "You were always that too, my King."

"Edward," the boy corrected him.

"My King," insisted the knight. "Until this quest is truly over."

About a Bracelet

It was Richard's second journey in a taxi, coming back from the hospital with Alex and Miles. They had got word via Milly who, in turn, had received word from Kit that the bracelet was on it's way to Weavers Fields. This was why the taxi was pulling up at that location.

The young prince held Miles's hand as Alex paid the driver. It felt odd, to Richard, to be in this place again, with such different circumstances. The man in the Apple costume was at the gate, handing out his flyers. The sun was bright, the day still quite hot. Miles pointed to the part of the field where the boys had first arrived in 2016.

"This is where it all started," he said. "With us three conspirators and the purple mist. Standing here, it's like it was yesterday."

Richard looked at him. "For me, it was yesterday."

They sat on the same bench where the boys had first met Amber. A balloon floated above them and away towards the railway bridge. It was another normal Summer day, to all appearances, but Richard and Miles felt the difference. There was something in the air.

A clown on a unicycle came along the path, surrounded by several children. He balanced himself and began to juggle coloured balls. Richard grinned, welcoming the entertainment. He leaned against Miles and watched for a while.

The clown cleverly shot the balls into a pocket and then brought out a small bunch of flowers. He looked dramatically puzzled for a moment, then screwed the flowers up into his hands. When he released his hands again he had a box of candy which he then shared with all the children.

Miles stood up, shook hands with the clown. He then took out his handkerchief, blew his nose and caused a spray of confetti. Miles winked at Richard who was staring in total amazement.

"How did you do that?" asked the prince.

Miles sat down again and tapped his nose. "Secret!" he said. "I had to learn a few tricks, to get by, over the years."

"He won't even tell me half of the things he knows," said Alex.

Richard watched the clown, and the following group of children, move on back along the park. Then he saw another child, a boy, running through the grass. It was John. The dung heap! He nudged Miles and pointed John out. He didn't quite understand all the message that had come through Milly but he understood enough, and Richard was still seething over the way the dung heap had locked him in.

Richard set off after him, judging the best angle to intercept him. They were both fast; too fast for Alex to stop the clash. It was not far from the stone where Richard tackled John. Two young boys clashing, making other people dodge out of their way.

Richard was on top, punching John repeatedly. "Slime bucket!" "Lizard!" "Dung breath!" "This is for my mother!" "Dungeon rat!" Richard was pounding all of his pent-up anger and frustration into John. It was not pretty. One ten years old boy knocking the stuffing out of another ten years old boy. Richard had taken John by surprise and winded him, so it was mostly Richard, and merciless. John was in tears, bruised and yelling. Other children had gattered around and were shouting encouragement.

Then strong hand dragged Richard off his prey. "Get off," demanded the prince. "Let me at him." He struggled, determined to finish the job. He landed Alex a punch in the nose before he realised what he was doing.

John wiped blood from his own nose and staggered away from Richard. He saw the stone and moved towards it. A purple mist began to form. Another pair of strong hands held on to him before he could go further. He looked up at Robert.

"Are you alright?" Robert asked him while keeping a tight hold of him.

"Yes, let me go."

"First let me check you over."

"No." John struggled, seeing the purple mist, desperate to reach the stone.

People were wondering about the mist, wondering about the boys, wondering about the men. Many phone cams were recording the incident. Kit appeared beside John and quickly slipped the bracelet off him.

John lurched to try catch hold of the bracelet but Kit held it too high for him. "You bast ..."

Robert put a hand over John's mouth. "Keep your peace,"

John kicked himself free and made another lunge for the bracelet. Kit sidestepped and then ran off towards one of the park gateways, John in pursuit. Robert followed on. Some of the crowd kept their cameras rolling.

Kit crossed the road, just ahead of John. None of them saw the van until it crashed into John. There was a squeal of brakes and many gasps from the crowd. The driver of the van got out, holding his head in his arms as he checked to see what he'd done.

The body of a young boy lay still and lifeless. Some cameras were still recording, but most had been turned off as people realised the impact. The driver turned away, inconsolable. Kit approached the body, knowing the story but unable to digest the ending.

Then it happened in front of them. The body of John became the body of a man. Daren Wolf who was now dead twice ... or not at all. The body faded and then was gone. The driver, who had been inconsolable, now turned to Kit.

"What do you think you are doing, Kid?" demanded the driver. "I could have killed you! Get off the road, you nut."

Kit, still quite amazed, crossed back to the park to join Robert. He waited until the van had driven off, then he breathed deep and clung to Robert. He saw life going on as normal around the park, as though nothing unusual had happened. The clown on his unicycle was still keeping people entertained. He looked up at Robert's face. "Do you understand anything about that?"

Robert shook his head. "I'm trying not to." He saw that Kit still had hold of the bracelet. He kept one arm around his young friend as they walked to rejoin the others.

∽

The bracelet was on a coffee table in the lounge. Arthur sniffed at it. Everyone had examined it and, now, they all looked at Edward. He, in turn, glanced from one member of their party to another. Ralph sitting next to Milly. Robert and Kit crouched on the floor together. Alex sitting in an easy chair. Richard balanced on Miles's lap, and Amber holding Edward's hand.

Edward picked up the bracelet. In some ways he admired it. In other ways he hated it. It was both powerful and frightening. It seemed to only have power when close to the stone in Weavers Field so, right now, it was just a bracelet.

"The temptation to use this magic could become too great, depending on the circumstances," he said. "It needs to be taken far away from the stone and maybe buried. And we all must swear to never tell anyone about our secret."

"Like anyone would believe us," muttered Milly. "I don't even believe it myself."

Amber touched the bracelet, then stroked Edward's hair. "It's like a weird dream. Are we sure it's over? Is Daren dead?"

Miles adjusted Richard on his lap. "There are going to be lots of questions which we will probably never answer. Whether Daren Wolf ever existed, I feel that he's out of our lives. At least so long as we have the bracelet."

"How do we know he only had one magic item?" asked Ralph. "I think it is unlikely that he will return, but I shall rest easier the more days go by."

"Indeed," said Robert.

"We just have to hope," said Edward. "I, for one, have had my fill of magic and adventures. It's been a bitter few weeks. I have known too much sorry." He looked at Amber and kissed her hand. "But I have found new joys too."

Richard climbed off Miles' lap and got on the floor to nuzzle Arthur. He did not want to talk right now, or to think about people or things that he will never see again. He could accept change if he was left to come to terms with it in his own way.

"May I suggest," said Ralph. "That we keep the bracelet in a strong box, in a secure place, for a couple of weeks. Then, if it's agreeable, Robert and I shall find a place, away from the city, where we can bury it."

Amber saw the clock on the wall and checked it against the time on her phone. "I know it probably sounds kinda trivial but, if I'm too late home, I might get grounded, so I have to go." She stood up and pulled Edward with her. "I hope you understand."

Ralph rose too. "My lady. I shall escort you. This has been a vexful day."

"I'll escort her," said Edward.

"Then, my King." He corrected himself. "Edward. I shall escort you both."

Amber put her finger to Edward's lips to silence his protest. "Thanks, Ralph. But give us a moment outside alone, okay?"

Ralph understood and watched them go outside. By the gate, they kissed, softly, then hugged. It was a long silent hug. No words were needed. The air was close with no breeze. Edward looked into her eyes. They were as deep as his love for her.

When they parted, at her door, a look was enough. She knew the emptiness within her would be filled tomorrow, when she saw him again. His life had been changed for all time, but she was a part of it now. The boy who had been born to be King, the eldest of the princes in the tower, was her boy, and he loved her.

Edward and Ralph held back until she had closed her door, then began their walk back to the house. It was a simple journey, which was good news for Edward as he suspected he would be following it often. He had little idea what this area had looked like in 1483, probably woodland or farmland. Now he looked at the distant 'Gherkin', rising taller than the buildings in his eyeline, and he knew he had to visit that place, preferably with Amber.

When they reached his own gate, Edward paused and said, "I do love her. It's not just the magic."

"Are you telling me or asking me?" asked Ralph.

"Both."

"Do you think it's real love?"

"Yes." He gazed at Ralph. "for certain."

"Then, that's what matters." Ralph put supportive a hand on the boy. "But, yes, I also think it is real love. No magic could be as strong as real love. But take it slowly. You're both young enough to do that."

Edward gave him a warm hug. "Thank you, Sir Ralph."

"Just Ralph."

"Oh, yes." Edward gave a faint smile. "But you will always a knight in my eyes."

"And you will always be King in mine."

"We will be alright, won't we?" asked Edward. "It's going to be very strange."

Ralph nodded. "Yes. You and Richard are both strong, and you have good friends."

They touched knuckles and Edward gave him another hug as a taxi pulled up. Megan helped the old man out. The old man studied the front of the building as Megan paid the driver. She smiled on seeing Edward still in Ralph's arms.

"It's good to know that knights of old had their sensitive side," she said. "I thought I'd see if I had brought the final piece of the puzzle."

They went inside. The old man scanned the lounge, the furniture, the paintings, the people and focused on Miles. He reached deep inside of his damaged memory. He drew closer the Miles. "I know you ... don't I?"

"Yes," confirmed Miles, with surprise. "And I thought I was the only one left." He opened a drawer and brought out his own pouch with the sign of Edward. "After all these years."

The old man nodded. "Yes," after all these years.!"

Edward went into the kitchen. The back door was open. Richard was sitting on the step, looking up at the sky where a plane is just visible. Edward joined him on the step.

"Are you alright, brother?" he asked.

Richard nodded. "I was just thinking about stuff."

"Are you sad that we are not going back?"

Richard plucked a blade of grass and played with it for a moment. "Yes, but not too much now." He leaned against his brother and they sat arm in arm. "I am a bit afraid but not as much as I was in The Tower."

"It's alright to be afraid," said Edward.

Richard remembered the sounds and confusion of their first hours in 2016. "I'm not afraid of things anymore. It's just not knowing what's going to happen now."

Edward hugged him closer. "That makes two of us," he admitted. "But this is not a bad place, when we give it a chance."

"I know." Richard saw that the plane had gone. He dropped the blade of grass on the ground. "Alex say that the people who fly planes are called pilots."

Edward smiled. "I know."

Richard watched a blackbird take off from a tree. He had always wondered what it would be like to fly. "I want to be pilot," he said.

The End ... of The Beginning.

Notes

Shaa - in the chapter **Bewitched**, refers to Ralph Shaa, a preacher who claimed that the Princes in The Tower were illegitimate.

St Matthew's Church – in the chapter **Bewitched**, Edward and Richard visit this church in Bethnal Green. It is C of E but, in 1483, all Christian churches were Catholic so the boys would not have known the difference. The clergy at St Matthew's sometimes refer to themselves as priests.

Half Ryal – in the chapter **Yesterday's Now**, a rare gold coin, introduced by Edward 4th.

Anne of Brittany – in the chapter **Yesterday's Now**, was promised in marriage to Edward in 1480. After Edward's disappearance, she became Queen consort of France in 1491.

Elizabeth Woodville – the mother of Edward and Edward, had eight other children by Edward 4th. After the disappearance of her sons from The Tower, she was given assurance, by Richard the 3rd, that she was not harmed. She got her revenge when Henry Tudor promised to marry her daughter, Elizabeth. Henry defeated Richard the 3rd and became King of England.

Richard of Shrewsbury – was married at age 4, to Anne Mowbray who was aged 5. It was most probably a marriage of convenience. Anne died when she was only 8. Richard, following an act of Parliament, inherited all of her property. Two years later, Richard disappeared from The Tower of London.

Also by
Paul Boon

Helstrip
A true story from eighteenth century York

One Last Christmas
A heart-warming story of a family Christmas in Yorkshire

Brittle Twigs
A collection of poetry

Floppy Hats and Cider
Poems and Photos.

The Old Grey Whistle
Poems and Sketches.

Printed in Poland
by Amazon Fulfillment
Poland Sp. z o.o., Wrocław